THE
FOOT OF
THE WALK
MURDERS

SIMPSON GREARS

The Foot of the Walk Murders

RYMOUR

© Simpson Grears 2020

ISBN 978-1-8381863-0-2

Published by Rymour Books
45 Needless Road,
PERTH
PH2 0LE

cover and book design by Ian Spring
printed by Imprint Digital, Exeter, Devon
set in Garamond 12/15

The paper used in this book is approved
by the Forest Stewardship Council

FSC

FOR EDINBURGH FRIENDS PAST AND PRESENT

AUTHOR'S NOTE

This book is a work of fiction and the characters and incidents portrayed are fictitious. If any characters resemble real Edinburgh people, past and present, then they (the real people) have probably given their permission. All murderers, fraudsters and other villains or unsavoury characters are, however, completely the product of the author's imagination.

Pubs, clubs, shops and other places portrayed are generally real and most of them still exist. A few, however. are partly or entirely fictitious.

The author is grateful to the many friends and colleagues who have helped to inspire, and have often commented on, these stories, but would like to specially mention the late Pat Clark, whose extensive knowledge of the detective genre was of great assistance, the late Keith Stewart, who read the first draft, and Alan Hellen, for his meticulous proofreading.

The cover features details from Michael McVeigh's *Edinburgh in the Festival* and Thomas Dolby's view of Edinburgh from a hot air balloon (1870).

CONTENTS

Through a Glass Darkly   9

A Maritime Mystery   22

Et in Arcadia Ego   38

The Fairy Cup of Dun Acainn   51

The Case of the Wrong Necklace   62

A Potato Riddle   70

The Foot of the Walk Murders   79

A Mysterious Affair at Gayfield House   109

The Spectator at the Hippodrome   127

The Premature Death of the Beautiful
   Grace Bonnington   137

The Black Redeemer   146

The King and Queen of Sheba   171

The Saint Bernard's Supporters Club   178

Spelling Lessons   189

The World Turned Upside Down   195

The First and Last Mystery   214

THROUGH A GLASS DARKLY

Detective Inspector Nigel Stonelaw had, by his own estimation, a good to very good success rate since his move to the Edinburgh and Lothians Police—a little short, however, of the excellence for which he had been renowned in his days with the Yorkshire Constabulary.

And now this new case perplexed him. The facts were simple. James Semple, the assistant keeper of oriental flora at the Royal Botanic Garden had been murdered last Friday—on the eve of a new exhibition devoted to the rare subcontinental strobilanthus ruberfolia, the red-flowering kurinji.

Semple, along with Sandy McFadyen, the head keeper of oriental flora, Margaret Anderson, a rather prim lady who was the Garden's chief librarian, Kevin Sweeney, the overseer of the greenhouses, and Alan Lorimer, a young botanist who had worked with Semple on the exhibition, had gone to the Northern Bar, near the east gate of the Garden, to celebrate the completion of the display.

After downing his third pint of beer, Semple had seemingly choked. Before he subsided into a coma from which he would not awake, he had been distinctly heard saying, 'The head keeper... the head keeper... ' The cause of death had almost immediately been established as the poisonous extract of the kurinji itself.

Subsequently, Sandy McFadyen had been arrested and

a motive had been established. McFadyen had been jealous of his assistant's success with his research into the recently discovered strobilanthus ruberfolia—research which had spawned several publications of international merit. When Semple had been invited to give the inaugural address for the exhibition rather than himself, he had exploded with fury in the presence of several senior colleagues, The case seemed cut and dried—there was clearly both motive and opportunity—and yet... it was too simple, too obvious! McFadyen had grimly denied any part in it and, for reasons more to do with instinct than investigation, he did not seem, in Stonelaw's eyes, to be of the murdering mien.

Neither had Stonelaw's interviews with the various parties involved been especially illuminating, McFadyen had his own reasons for his sunken demeanour, Margaret Anderson had been too tearful and confused by the whole thing and didn't seem to remember much about the evening at all. And Kevin Sweeney... well, Kevin Sweeney had certainly been one of the most difficult interviewees Stonelaw ever remembered encountering. He was, by turns, both belligerent and sanctimonious. Both berating the botanists at the Garden for their petty obsessions and incompetence and spouting seemingly pious observations on life in general. He didn't seem unduly upset about Semple's death. 'Ach,' he said, 'a bairn's first breath's the beginning o' his death.' When asked who he thought might be responsible for the death he had wagged his finger, drawing his rather splenetic bearded face close to Stonelaw's, and had said 'Mark my words, a crackit bell ne'er will mend!' At this point Stonelaw, completely perplexed, had ended the interview.

And Alan Lorimer... in fact, Stonelaw had not been able

to interview Alan Lorimer at all! Lorimer had left the pub just before Semple's death and, seemingly unaware of the incident had left the next morning on a field trip to the subcontinent. Stonelaw was still, through the Indian police, trying to trace him.

So then Stonelaw had raised his doubts with Chief Superintendent Robert Ord. Ord had been a major investigator in his own day, known for his solutions to the Radical Road Rapist and the Murders in the Speculative Club affairs, but these days, awaiting retirement, he mostly concerned himself with historical cases and his editing and annotation of William Roughead's *Scottish Trials*. His walrus moustache and his habit of puffing furiously on a reeking pipe on his way out of the office had even compelled some of the younger members of the force to nickname him PC Murdoch, after a character in the 'Oor Wullie' comic strip. No-one, however, had ever dared to call him it to his face. Stonelaw negotiated his way up the winding staircase to Ord's attic office. An office Ord had always preferred with its panoramic views of the Edinburgh skyline-looking out over his patch like Chaucer overseeing the gates of London.

'Does Inspector Rubrik share your doubts?' Ord asked.

'I'm afraid he's very busy on a case down at Leith Docks', Stonelaw replied. The last thing he wanted was his chief rival involved. Stonelaw hadn't taken at all to Inspector Rubrik since his arrival in Scotland. He thought him boorish and arrogant and, once or twice, he thought, he had come across him making fun of his Yorkshire accent.

'Well then, why not ask Hamish McDavitt?', Ord had suggested, I'm sure that he'd let you buy him a dram.'

Stonelaw had vaguely heard of McDavitt, ex-archivist of

the Lauriston Castle collection, prominent member of the Old Town Century Club, bon viveur and expert on Scottish malt whisky—one of an endless line of Edinburgh eccentrics that everyone seemed to have heard of, or know, or know a good friend of, or know an extraordinary story about. There was what might be called the lunatic fringe: Mad Maura, the Skull or the Rat Woman of Forrest Road, then there were the merely eccentric: the Eminent Professor, the King of Scotland or the Master without Honour. McDavitt certainly belonged to the latter group and was, Stonelaw had heard, generally kindly thought-of in the village community that consisted of the clubs and bars of central Edinburgh. Nevertheless, his relevance to this particular case was not clear to him.

'I don't see how an old man with no detective experience can solve a complicated case over a glass of whisky?

'Still, I suggest you try it, laddie.'

Peevishly, then, Stonewall had agreed to meet McDavitt in the Scotch Malt Whisky Society in Leith and some time later he had arrived there.

He had driven down through the town. Past Waverley Station, the site of an early Physic Garden, moved from the fields at Holyrood, where healing herbs for local physicians had been grown among the fulsome smells of the Fleshmarket, the smoke and bustle and stinking sewers of old Edinburgh; down Leith Walk, to where the Physic Garden had been removed to become Edinburgh's first Botanic Garden—once rural fields but now overbuilt with tenement and shops.

Then, on impulse, or perhaps to focus his mind a little more, he had taken a little detour to stop at the Royal Botanic Garden itself, in Inverleith, and he had strolled a little amongst the trees and rock gardens. His perambulation was, typically, a pleasant Sunday outing for most Edinburgh folk, but the

Botanic Garden also, he realised, constituted a long tradition of endeavour and scholarship in the natural sciences that had marked this city since the Enlightenment. It was a pleasant, perhaps idyllic setting, but now, suddenly, within this sheltered haven, there was a premature death and an unpleasant mystery to solve.

He wandered through the peat garden, around the duck pond and as far as Inverleith House with its fine panorama of the central Edinburgh skyline. Then down through the palm and orchid and cycad hothouses and finally to the exhibition centre with its walls dedicated to the deadly red kurinji. After twenty minutes or so he had accumulated some sweat on his brow, a little knowledge of garden environments and the history of plants and botany but, he had to admit, no further insight into why such a placid setting should inspire a cruel and sudden murder.

The Malt Whisky Society was entered via an old stone stairway at the back of a rather obscure warehouse building just off the Shore at Leith. The sitting room was airy and comfortable with its vaulted ceiling and cracked leather Chesterfield sofas.

McDavitt himself was a lanky man with a slight stoop and a whole head of slightly unkempt greying hair whose rather quaint dress could have been described as 'dapper', but was just a little too carelessly arranged. He wore a standard dress suit, an unbuttoned waistcoat and a tie rather loosely arranged in a double knot which featured some insignia that Stonelaw did not recognise. The most noble feature of McDavitt was his head, which seemed a little too large for his body and featured two widely spaced large deep blue eyes with a piercing direct look. This, at first perhaps, gave him a rather fierce look, but, on greeting, a twinkle in his eyes, a disarming smile and, above all, his gentle, rather sing-song and slightly accented voice, demonstrated McDavitt's ability to put all his acquaintances at immediate ease. (Much later, Stonelaw would discover that McDavitt's calm, sweet-sounding and reasoned diction could also disguise an inner passion and conviction.)

After a few preliminary greetings, they were seated with their drinks. While Stonelaw had been happy to stick to a bottle of Caledonian eighty-shilling ale, McDavitt had perused an elaborate menu to choose a malt from cask 2206.

'Hmm, a very dark concoction, matured in oak barrels used for tawny port. The pungency of macaroon bars and old steam trains,' McDavitt had commented, his nose halfway into the tasting glass, ' …but quite a floral finish, like a tight knit bunch of slightly faded red roses.' He took a long lingering sip from the brim. 'Now, Inspector Stonelaw, I presume that have come to see me about the distasteful events at the Garden?

'How do you know that?' Stonelaw was surprised.

'It wasn't difficult. I generally read the newspapers and I presume that a gratuitous murder in such a tranquil setting will exercise the minds of you and your colleagues… and …' He leaned forward and brushed his hand across Stonelaw's jacket. ' …I can only presume you have been there recently as there are fallen petals of the elderflower blossom on your shoulders.' He rubbed a little substance between his fingers.

'It should smell of bananas but some say that it smells like cat's pee at this time of year. I hope you don't intend to brew any wine from it!

Once the subject of their meeting was established, McDavitt

asked Stonelaw to describe as best he could the histories of the characters involved and their actions on the night in question. Stonelaw, with years of experience in dealing with straightforward facts had summarised succinctly by the time McDavitt had downed his dram.

Sandy McFadyen was five years short of retirement from his post but there had been some suspicions that he was losing his authority in the department. He had behaving somewhat indiscreetly for a member of senior management and, on the occasion of the murder, it was suspected that he had been drinking earlier in the day.

Margaret Anderson had also been behaving strangely. There was talk of a broken love affair and recently, it seemed, she had developed quite a crush on young Lorimer, regarded as a little unseemly in an older woman. She had taken Semple's death very badly and had seemingly been mostly in tears and unable to speak to anyone since.

Alan Lorimer was an anglo-Indian and an acolyte of Semple, who had supervised his PhD which he had obtained at the age of only 22. He had been the youngest botanist ever appointed by the Garden and with his handsome tawny good looks and moneyed background—his family owned a tea plantation in southern India—he had been the envy of most of his colleagues who thought that he had ambitions beyond his current status.

Kevin Sweeney, Stonelaw had discovered, had been in quite a bellicose mood of late, but it was quickly established that he was constantly of this demeanour. Although he worked with academics on a daily basis, he viewed them with faintly disguised disdain. There had been the makings of an argument with Semple that night in the Northern Bar about something to do with temperature control in the boiler room.

On the fatal night, they had left the Garden at about 6.00pm—although Lorimer had stayed behind a little to shut down the exhibition room and check the plants. They had walked to the Northern Bar where the first round had be purchased: beer for the men and a gin and tonic for Miss Anderson. There were two more rounds but Lorimer had finished his final pint quickly as he had to pack for a short period of leave he had booked in order to see his parents and undertake some field work. Shortly afterwards, Semple had collapsed. Sweeney had attempted vigorously to revive him before the ambulance came but shortly after arrival at the hospital he was pronounced dead. Two barmaids and other customers had distinctly heard Semple's last words and, when the cause of death had been established, there had been no choice but to immediately arrest McFadyen.

'I've been through it in my head several times, Mr McDavitt. Lorimer didn't seem to have anything to gain, being so junior in his position. Sweeney is a hothead but surely had no real substance to his disagreement with Semple. I thought about Miss Anderson. Women can have deep passions. Perhaps she was having a secret affair with Semple. But why was she so upset at his death? Which brought me obviously to think of suicide—but why? So, only McFadyen seemed to have a real motive, although just a storm in a teacup over some academic gobbledegook!'

'You shouldn't dismiss academic practices, Inspector', Hamish interjected. 'Even though the concerns of academia may seem trivial to the public at large, they themselves may engage in them with passion and obsession.'

'So you think McFadyen's motive is genuine?'

'The motive maybe, but perhaps not the conclusion… ' He thought for a moment. Has McFadyen been co-operative?'

'Well, that's another thing. McFadyen has other things on his mind at the moment.'

'What! Things more important than being accused of murder?'

'Well, *yes*, unfortunately, McFadyen is terminally ill. At most a year to live. Bone cancer, very painful. It came out after he was arrested. Seems he hadn't told his wife and family. It's all been quite a shock for them. Everyone was in tears, just like Margaret Anderson.'

McDavitt suddenly seemed curiously silent. He had tipped his head backward and was staring at the ceiling in a distracted way.

'Do you see something that we've missed?'

'Hmm', McDavitt mused, once again focusing his attention on Stonelaw. 'Perhaps I was just reflecting on the impetuosity of youth and the foolishness of middle age'. He shrugged. I fear that I have to recommend something that I rarely do, hut it might illuminate this little mystery. Inspector, I think we might have a pint of beer, in the Northern Bar.

As they drove to the pub, McDavitt had gazed out of the window towards the perimeter of the Botanic Garden.

Suddenly he said a few words: 'Margaret, are you grieving, o'er Goldengrove unleaving? Leaves, like the things of man, you with your fresh thoughts care for… '

Stonelaw was completely perplexed. As McDavitt seemed prepossessed, he cleared his throat.

'Oh, Inspector, my apologies, just a snatch of poetry that came into my head. Gerald Manley Hopkins, a strange chiel,

17

but a great poet.' He looked at Stonelaw. 'Are you fond of poetry yourself?'

But before Stonelaw could discourse on his knowledge of poetry, which was extremely limited indeed, they were at the bar of the Northern, a neat hostelry on a corner in Inverleith Row, with arched windows and a green façade featuring hanging baskets of hop. blossoms. McDavitt introduced Stonelaw to a new local ale called 'The Flowers of Edinburgh', a dark porter with a frothy top. They sat at a window table with their pints.

'So, Mr McDavitt. Do you have an idea?'

'I think so, Inspector, but first please call me Hamish! Everyone else does.'

He raised his pint glass so that the light from the window caught in it. 'Now, let's just sit here for a moment and enjoy our pint but at the same time let's think of what might have occurred on the night of the unfortunate death.' He had a good look around the bar, and Stonelaw followed his eyes, and then focused on McDavitt staring deeply into the glass of dark ale.

'Firstly, I imagine that they would choose this very ale, what is more appropriate than a beer named after their profession. It is on special offer and it comes in a glass specially designed for a renowned local brewery. Miss Anderson would receive her drink first and, seated, she could observe the barmaid pulling the frothy pints. As there were four pints for each round, it would take two trips to the table to deliver them.'

'On these occasions, though not exactly a formality, the head of department would probably buy the first round, his assistant the second. Then, I imagine, Lorimer the third, ahead of Sweeney, who was non-salaried, and Miss Anderson.

'Then, the murder. A drop of the lethal poison slipped into the beer. Semple topples the pint and… ' He hesitated.

'Why don't you try it, Inspector?'

Stonelaw hesitated. He imagined he could almost taste the bitterness of a lethal poison in the malty brew. But then he cleared his head and finished the beer in one last draught.

'Now what exactly do you see, Inspector?'

Stonelaw had raised the glass up to the light to finish his pint. Suddenly, he saw the point!

'The headkeeper!'

'Yes! I thought a beer-drinking man like yourself would know that! Each pint glass or tumbler has a little indented pattern on its base that is supposed to help keep the head on the beer. It is called the headkeeper.' And this particular glass has the symbol of the brewery, three wheatsheafs, engraved on its base. The last thing that Semple would have seen before he collapsed, the symbol of a very old Edinburgh brewery. Its name is staring at us from the font on the bar.'

Stonelaw gazed at the bar. 'Lorimer's!'

'Indeed, another old Edinburgh institution, founded in Dalry in 1854. The brewery still stands. The very last conscious memory Semple retained was that of the name of his murderer. Whether it was callously planned or just serendipity I don't know, I suspect the former.'

'But what was the motive?'

'The very motive you suggested yourself—academic jealousy. The red-flowering kurinji is a plant from southern India. I suspect Lorimer discovered it, or at least a new variation of it. His PhD was fast-tracked and his position at the Garden ensured, but at a cost. Semple would take the credit—it is a not uncommon academic tactic. Lorimer

19

couldn't reveal the truth without discrediting himself. Bur he was ambitious and impetuous, On the day of the murder he snapped, some inner rage possessed him. He was, I suspect, a very narcissistic young man, totally obsessed with himself and totally without a conscience. He probably had been brought up to think he could get away with anything he wanted to do. He stayed behind to extract the poison, inserted it into the beer then left—smugly assuming his plot had ended perfectly, as it did seem to do.'

Stonelaw though for a moment, going over the facts in his head in the careful manner he had been trained to always apply. At last he spoke. 'I'm sure you're right, McDavitt… Hamish, I mean. The facts all fit. I've come across criminals like Lorimer, but only very rarely, Narcissistic Personality Disorder, the boffins call it. Don't care for anything except themselves and don't consider the consequences of what they do.' He shook his head and released a long slow breath, as if relieved of a great burden. 'Well, thank God you've revealed the truth, and saved an innocent man.'

McDavitt smiled. 'I doubt if my little intervention has made any difference at all to the fate of the unfortunate accused. You see, the conclusion of the little poem I thought of earlier also reveals a fundamental truth about mankind. Slowly, carefully enunciating the words, he concluded the verse: ' …Now no matter, child, the name: sorrow's springs are the same; it is the blight man was born for, it is Margaret you mourn for… '

'Margaret? Are you thinking of Miss Anderson?'

'Yes, her over-reaction to Semple's death struck me. Sometimes when we grieve for others, it is also for ourselves. She was herself growing old, and she had made a fool of herself with Lorimer, who no doubt found the whole thing very amusing in his own callous way. But never underestimate

20

the foolish obsessions of middle-age. Margaret Anderson was sitting at the table and watching Lorimer's every action. I suspect that she saw everything and, in a little while, whatever happens, she will get over the shock and tell you what she knows.'

'And Lorimer has escaped.'

'Perhaps, but I suggest you check out Munnar, the tea town in Kerala. Not only the finest tea in India grows there but also the blue-flowering kurinji, which flowers only once in every twelve years. It is due in October this year and no doubt Lorimer won't want to miss it.'

'But how do you know that?'

'Elementary, really. Last week I was out for a stroll and I simply went to the exhibition hall at the Garden, as you did, and I read the placards accompanying the exhibits.'

Stonelaw shook his head. 'It all seems so obvious now you explain, yet I never thought... ' He looked at McDavitt then down at the table. 'But, Hamish, you haven't touched your beer.'

'Filthy stuff, Inspector, and I'm not surprised no good has come of it... and if you weren't a Sassenach yourself you would know what the flowers of Edinburgh used to mean!'

A beam of sunlight broke through then window of the bar and illuminated the gantry. Hamish's face broke into a smile.

'Ah, I think I spy there, on the highest shelf, a twenty-five year old Dalwhinnie, from the highest distillery in Scotland. Perhaps the occasion calls for a wee dram... '

A MARITIME MYSTERY

Hamish McDavitt was extremely fond of his top floor flat in Royal Terrace. Royal Terrace was the first of three Georgian terraces that snaked around Calton Hill. the east end of Edinburgh city centre: Royal Terrace, Regent Terrace and Carlton Terrace. Calton Hill itself had had a long history before it became an integral part of John Playfair's plan to create Edinburgh's New Town, often known, because of its classicism, as the Modern Athens. Once it had been extensively wooded and there was evidence of strange goings-on; ancient faery and witch cults and even human sacrifices on the hillside itself! Today, capped with the old observatory, several other buildings and the National Monument—an incomplete version of the Parthenon in Athens, built to scale from old grey sandstone but never completed—it was a place for children to play and fly kites on windy Edinburgh days, or for tourists to obtain a remarkable vista of Edinburgh.

Indeed it was here, one day in the eighteenth century, perusing the view from the top of the hill, that an Irishman, Robert Barker, had invented the panorama, a complete one hundred and eighty view drawn or painted in a dome (another, probably apocryphal, story was that he got the idea from the long narrow windows in Calton Jail where he was imprisoned for debt).

Royal Terrace was a very grand terrace indeed, high on the

north side of Calton Hill overlooking the east New Town, Leith Walk and, further afield, the docks at Leith and the Firth of Forth. Centuries ago it would have been a superb vantage point to see the ships coming into the port. And the sea route was, indeed, the route which nearly all visitors to Edinburgh would have taken until the nineteenth century and the advent of the steam engine. On his wall Hamish had a framed print of Munster's view of Edinburgh, sketched from a ship approaching Leith in around 1580, showing church spires, houses and a crazed cacophony of rocks representing Arthur's Seat and the Castle Hill.

Yes, the houses in Royal Terrace were very grandiose, their doorways buttressed by Doric pilasters. Once these were townhouses and the homes of the gentry or of successful merchants. Indeed, Royal Terrace had once been known as Whisky Row, because of the preponderance of successful distillers who lodged there. Now most were converted to hotels or individual flats. At number 30, Hamish had the smallest, the attic apartment, but it was by all means commodious enough for his needs. Hamish had worked hard to be able to afford this flat, accumulating his salary as archivist of the Lauriston Castle Collection for several years., What it had cost would have bought a much larger house on the outskirts of Edinburgh or in West Lothian, but Hamish, a single man, had everything he needed and, for him, the greatest treasure was to be a part of Edinburgh history.

So, Hamish liked living here for the view, the easy access to Calton Hill and the Old and New Towns, but most of all he loved the history of the area and the houses. In fact, at one time, in this very terrace lived men whose vision encompassed the spectacular vista from the top of the hill and much more.

Next door to Hamish not one but two of the adjacent townhouses had once been owned by a remarkable man, Professor Charles Sarolea. Sarolea, who was the author of numerous books and pamphlets and, it was reputed, spoke twenty-two languages, needed the space for his library— the largest private collection of books owned by a private individual ever! Sarolea had lived well into the twentieth century but had been denounced as a Nazi-sympathiser during World War Two. Now his books were gone and his houses split and disposed to buyers who possibly knew nothing of his great collection. Also, nearby, had once lived other remarkable gentlemen: Charles Piazza Smyth, once Astronomer Royal for Scotland and the first person to photograph inside the pyramids. And John Bartholomew, the famous map maker had lived in another townhouse nearby.

Hamish thought of them all and of their maps and plans whenever we looked out of his window. Here he could see part of the east New Town, laid out as planned, and the ghosts of other streets that never had been built because, in the mid-nineteenth century, the merchants had largely switched their money to developments in the West End, at the other end of Princes Street. His eye could follow the snaking lines of Leith Walk and Easter Road that connected the city with its port at Leith. Here fishwives would ascend to the city centre with their weighty creels of newly caught fish on their shoulders, carts and carriages would transport passengers and goods from the shipping office and ships at the docks. Once, a railway line, long gone, had gone back and forth to Granton and Newhaven, coming from an underground tunnel between Waverley Station and Scotland Street. Hamish had always thought that the feats of Victorian engineers were quite extraordinary.

Today, in fact, Hamish had planned a walk down part of the old railway line to Newhaven—now a foot and cycle path—to the Harbour Bar where he would lunch with the editor of the *Playfair Review* to discuss a proposed article on the long defunct Edinburgh football team, St Bernard's. In anticipation of a day by the sea he had laid out a blazer with a yachting club crest and his St Kilda Society puffin tie and badge. However, the morning had not gone quite as smoothly as he had anticipated.

'Nonsense,' said Lynn Landemar, 'It's the middle of summer and it's a heatwave! You're not dressing up like an old fuddy-duddy. I'll look out a short-sleeved shirt and some casual trousers.'

Lynn was Hamish's sometime housekeeper and, he found, was increasingly taking an interest in his attire, buying him shorts and ties from car boot sales and charity shops. His wardrobes were getting alarmingly full. For Hamish, whose personal view was that no-one needed more than two of any garment, this was quite disconcerting.

'But,' objected Hamish, 'the Edinburgh weather is notably unreliable. Four seasons in one day, they say. I had better be prepared.'

Lynn frowned a little and shook her head slowly in a manner that suggested that this argument was not going to sway her at all.

Meanwhile Detective Inspector Nigel Stonewall was driving up Ferry Road on his return to his office in Torpichen Street. He was unusually thoughtful. The case he had been working on was not pleasant. Hard drugs. As big a problem in Edinburgh as in most large cities. Drug addicts weren't hard to find in Edinburgh. Lost people, with a peculiar vacancy behind their eyes. Sometimes they would be picked up shoplifting or trying to snatch handbags in town. As often as not they would just be wandering the streets and shops of the estates. It was difficult to know what could be done for them.

In fact, drug dealers weren't particularly hard to find either. In many a housing block in Muirhouse or Niddrie, there would be flats with reinforced doors, often with several locks. They were often battered from kicks or hammer blows. Sometimes they had obscene graffiti written on them. They had no letterbox or nameplate. These were the haunts of dealers. But they were not easy to access unless you knew something about them. Even if the police could gain access and had a search warrant, the dealers were slippery and had numerous ways of disposing off or hiding the goods.

Nigel had been working on a drugs case for a couple of weeks. And, just a couple of days ago, he had thought they were on to something. Perhaps something big. Perhaps even something to match the spectacular coup that the Glasgow and Argyll police had pulled off a couple of months ago—a major cache of raw cocaine found on a fishing boat in Arran! A couple of well-known Glasgow gangsters were likely to go down on that one.

Unfortunately in this case, however, the tip-off that his department had received had, surprisingly, come to nothing. The whole business perplexed him. It was a puzzle, he thought, that required some reflection, rather than more walking the streets of housing schemes. So, when he got back to his desk, he decided to telephone Hamish McDavitt.

After some negotiation with Lynn, Hamish was lacing his light canvas shoes in preparation for his walk down to Newhaven when he heard the telephone. However, when Stonelaw had outlined the case he was investigating, he changed his plans, cancelled his luncheon engagement and, instead, arranged to meet Stonelaw in the Old Dock Bar in Leith.

Leith was a particularly interesting bit of Edinburgh, thought Stonelaw, as he drove down through Constitution Street into Commercial Street, passing the solid Victorian office buildings that once housed the merchant banks and shipping offices at the heart of the once thriving port. Now many were converted into restaurants or housing; down by the docks themselves there was more housing and a massive shopping centre beside which was moored the Queen's yacht Britannia. Leith was still a commercial centre, but dedicated more to the leisure industry than the shipping commerce of its industrial heyday.

Nevertheless, the Leith docks still had their fair share of shipping, and it was concerning that activity that Stonelaw had first received a tip-off regarding drug smuggling, The intelligence branch of the CID had intercepted a coded message which suggested that the Esperance—a freight vessel that plied a trade around between the east coast of Scotland and ports on the North Sea, mostly delivering aggregate for road surfacing—was arriving from Denmark with a contraband cargo of Class A narcotics concealed aboard The ship had been cleared by customs, but when it docked at Prince Albert Dock, a team from the Drug Squad had been waiting. They had boarded the ship, searched the crew and then, methodically, began to search the ship. They thought they had cracked it when they discovered in the galley, under a sink, a dozen cartons of, supposedly, washing powder.

However, on examination it turned out that it was precisely what it claimed to be—detergent. Further inspection of the ship, though extremely thorough, had failed to find anything illicit at all.

Stonelaw explained all this to Hamish at the Old Dock Bar, a pleasant and substantial hostelry down near the King's Wark—where George IV had landed and been greeted by Sir Walter Scott in 1823. The Old Dock had been a public house since 1813, just before the Battle of Waterloo and was a fine old building with thick stone walls and teak beams. It was now flanked by a rather superior seafood restaurant and was altogether a much more genteel place than when foreign sailors and merchant seamen caroused there.

Hamish had arrived—having, for the most part, won his battle with Lynn—in his St Kilda puffin tie and, for good measure, sporting a lapel badge commemorating the Ben Line—famous ships that once sailed from Leith all over the world. They sat by the window and Hamish had insisted that they each had a Laphraoig, a particularly pungent whisky from the Isle of Islay on the west coast of Scotland. 'It gets its slight iodine flavour from the ware, or seaweed, that is still gathered from the shore near the distillery', Hamish explained. 'but it has a deeper essence to it; echoes of the cry of the sea-mauk or the sensation of the fresh Atlantic sea mist settling in the air after a sudden squall has blown its course.'

Stonelaw, who found the malt a little too pungent for his taste, changed the subject. 'So we found nothing at all. Perhaps the tip-off was just a huge mistake.'

Hamish's brow furrowed a little. 'I don't think so,' he said.

'Why not?' enquired Stonelaw.

'Well, the packets of detergent, for one thing. It seems far too many for any sensible purpose. I suggest it was there deliberately, to mislead your men, in case the crew needed time to secrete or offload something else.'

'And yet our search was thorough. Nothing at all was found. If the contraband was on board the ship, and our intelligence insists it was, how was it spirited ashore?'

Hamish had a rather distant look. He finished his whisky and rose from his seat, spending a minute or two examining the hydrographic charts, paintings and prints of old ships on the wall of the bar. One framed object caught his interest.

'Look at this, Nigel,' he said. 'This is an old charter from the early eighteen hundreds. See, it gives to one John McAvoy, his family and descendants the sole right to all moorings and liveries on the shores of Granton and Leith.'

'Sounds familiar,' said Stonelaw. 'We interviewed the Association of Leith Boatmen. I'm sure that it was a McAvoy that I spoke to.'

Hamish looked thoughtful. 'There are very old maritime traditions that still hold sway today.' He gave himself a shake, as if to come back to the present day from a dream of the past. 'However,' he said, in a positive tone, 'the fact is that we are no nearer solving your problem. Do you think that maybe we should go down to the dock for a look around?'

They got down to the docks and there was the Esperance, still moored at a deserted dock. 'Although we couldn't find anything', Nigel explained, 'we managed to note some minor discrepancies in maritime law. Enough to insist that the vessel wasn't going anywhere for a while.' They walked up to the edge of the jetty and looked up at the rather shabby and slightly rusting vessel. 'Do you want to see on board? I can call the Harbourmaster.'

'Not particularly,' replied Hamish. 'I'm sure that your men have thoroughly searched the interior. Besides I have to admit that, although I like the coastline and the traditions of the sea, sailing vessels are a bit too claustrophobic for me. Didn't Dr Johnson say that going to sea was like being in prison with the additional risk of drowning?'

'However,' he added, 'One question. After the ship had moored, your men were instructed not to let anything or anyone leave the vessel?'

'Absolutely, they are all highly trained at setting out an exclusion zone and conducting a search.'

'Exclusion zone? That means also that nothing and no-one—apart from your men, of course—was allowed on to or off of the vessel?'

'Yes, of course. Why?'

Hamish walked over to a bollard, one of three on this part of the dock. 'And this is where the ship was secured?'

'Yes, but what are you getting at?'

Hamish frowned and screwed up his face in a way that usually showed that he was thinking deeply. 'Look, Nigel,' he said, pointing at a timber-built building some way up the dock. Isn't that the office of the Leith Boatmen?'

'I think it is,' said Nigel. 'Don't know if there is anyone there but.'

'Oh, I think so,' said Hamish. 'In fact, from the sun glinting on a lens just inside the window, I suspect we are being watched very closely.'

They approached the office and rang a bell. The door

was opened by a rather surly looking gentleman, of medium height, wearing a fisherman's jersey and green Wellington boots.

'Mr McAvoy?' asked Hamish.

The man seemed suspicious, looking at them both in turn, and eventually spoke slowly and deliberately. 'What exactly are you after? I've already spoken at length to your companion. Surely you cannot believe that our corporation is involved in any way in shady goings-on?'

Hamish took him aside and gave him a smile and a conspiratorial look. 'Oh no, not at all, not at all. I've always been an admirer of the shipshape way you run your operation down here. My uncle, you know, was a seafarer himself.'

Stonelaw suddenly saw that Hamish had a hip flask in his hand. 'You wouldn't care for a wee special dram. A twenty-year-old Port o' Leith. I've been keeping a little for when I had a chance to come down here again.' McAvoy looked more relaxed. 'Not when I'm on duty, of course,' he said, shaking his head. Then he looked over his shoulder. 'But on the other hand, I think I see my brother just coming down the quay to relieve me.'

When they had had a dram, Hamish asked him, 'Maybe we can just go over again what happened when the Esperance moored here the other day. You were there, weren't you?'

'Yes, of course, we don't miss anything that happens here. That's our job. But this time the police were there too, It's not the first time we've had the police or the customs meet a ship. Naturally, we co-operate fully with them.'

'And this time, when the ship was moored, was it just the same way as usual.'

'Och, yes, just as usual.'

'Can you describe it to us?'

'It's simple. The lock boys from the Forth Port caught the heaving line with the monkey's fist. Then they put the eye of the mooring line on the bollard and attached it to the drum at the winch. Then, in a minute or two, the ship was berthed.'

'And did you or your men do anything at all?'

'Just inspected the mooring to ensure it was OK. The police wanted to get on as quickly as possible.'

'So you didn't speak to the crew of the Esperance at all?'

'Not on this occasion.'

'But would you usually speak to the crew?'

'Och, yes. Often enough, if we need any more information for the log, or to ask them where they want the heaving line.'

Hamish eyes suddenly lit up. 'Nigel,' he said, 'I may have a solution to your problem after all!'

'Well, what is it then,' said Nigel, who had been rather bored by this conversation but now seemed more lively.

'Well, when I was a boy, in Anstruther. I used to go down to the harbour to see the fishing boats come in, and sometimes bigger trawlers or freezer ships. My uncle used to explain to me about the ports he'd been to and how boats and ships were moored.'

'The way that boats are moored, I think, is roughly like this—correct me if I'm wrong, Mr McAvoy. The crew would throw a rope on to the jetty. This rope, however, consisted of two parts: the heaving line, a lightweight rope which was attached to the heavier mooring line. It would have a knot called a monkey's fist at one end, sometimes weighed down by a bolt. It could give you a sore hit if you got in the way of it. The mooring line, however, would be the anchor, wound round the bollard. The heaving line would then be detached and usually thrown back on to the boat.'

Nigel suddenly saw the point.

'But the heaving line, in this case, wasn't thrown back aboard, or we would have noticed because something would have entered our exclusion zone!'

'Is that correct, Mr McAvoy?'

'It is, indeed. It would simply have been left at the bollard, to be collected later.'

'And,' said Hamish, 'even though the heaving line is a fairly lightweight rope, there would still be plenty of room to stuff something in the core of it!'

At around 6.30pm that evening, Hamish answered the telephone. It was Nigel Stonelaw.

'Unfortunately, there was no sign of the missing heaving line anywhere on the ship or the quay, just a few particles of rope. The initial forensic tests proved inconclusive as well. There were some traces of unusual chemicals on the rope particles, but we couldn't positively associate them with illegal substances, and these ropes have possibly been to so many different destinations anyway.'

'So', said Hamish, 'it looks as if the ingenious drug smugglers may have defeated us this time.'

'It looks that way,' said Nigel, with a sigh of exasperation. 'However, we may have a new lead. Special Branch have picked up a scrap of a communication encoded into an email message. It was directed to Edinburgh, as far as we know, and was sent earlier this morning.'

'And what does it say?'

'Just a few words: 'Collect goods. . . midnight… take special care… Scotland Yard. . . ' Nigel stopped for a moment to let

Hamish assimilate the message.

'Of course,' he continued, 'we immediately got on to Scotland Yard. We thought they might have received some sort of tip off. But they knew nothing of any drugs deal, or anything to do with Edinburgh.' There was another moment's silence.

'What do you think?'

If Stonelaw had been able to see Hamish McDavitt at that as screwed up in an almost grotesque posture that denoted he was thinking very deeply indeed.

'Nigel,' Hamish eventually replied. 'Can you come here right away. But alone... and bring your own car, not a police car. Pick me up outside my place in about twenty minutes.'

'But I don't know if I can get away.' Stonelaw protested. 'Everyone's a bit agitated around here after the message.'

'Trust me,' said Hamish, 'It will only take about an hour of your time... and I might have something interesting to show you!'

Twenty five minutes later, when Stonelaw pulled up in Royal Terrace, he was astonished at what he encountered. Firstly, Hamish was dressed in a short-sleeved Hawaiian shirt with mottled coloured patterns and, almost unbelievably, a pair of khaki shorts revealing hairy legs perched on sandalled feet accompanied by turned down creamy white socks. Also, he found that Hamish was not alone but accompanied by two schoolgirls of about 12-14 years of age sitting on the steps about Hamish's flat, looking quite sullen and bored.

'You're late', said one of them as he got out of the car.

'We don't have all day you know', said the other, 'There's a rock concert on the telly, direct from the Millennium Stadium in Cardiff.'

'Cardiff is very *now*,' said the first one.

'What on earth… ' started Stonelaw.

'Ah, this is Belinda and this is Jade—Belinda and Jade Landemar', said Hamish. I've borrowed them.'

'Oh,' said Nigel.

'And we're really too big to go out to play', said Belinda, the elder of the two, who had been first to speak.

'But', said Hamish, 'You're not too big for the magazines and the ice cream I promised you, are you?'

Stonelaw was looking completely lost.

'Don't worry. Just come with us for half an hour and all will become clear.'

They drove through Gayfield Square past the police station, along London Street and around Drummond Square by the bluish bronze plaque to the poet Sidney Goodsir Smith and turned right into Scotland Street. Hamish instructed Stonelaw to park halfway down the street on the left, between a mini and an enormous American car with sideboards that looked like something from the days of Al Capone. Nigel looked at it curiously. 'Don't worry,' said Hamish, 'I know the owner, he's a member of the Malt Whisky Society and a fine connoisseur of the cratur!'

Stonelaw was still bewildered but acquiesced a bit grudgingly when Hamish asked him to take off his jacket and tie and roll up his shirt sleeves. They walked to the bottom of the street where, beneath a stone wall there was a sharp dip down to a children's play

'This is it,' said Hamish.

'This is what?' enquired Stonelaw.

'Scotland Yard, of course! At the bottom of Scotland

Street. The subject of your intercepted message. Nothing to do with London. That was just an assumption you made.'

'Oh!' Suddenly Stonelaw realised his mistake. He looked agitated. 'Perhaps I should call the office?'

'No. No,' said Hamish. 'If this is the site of the drug drop there is a good chance it is being watched. That's why we're dressed like typical New Town parents out for a stroll in the sun with the children.'

Stonelaw looked Hamish up and down. If there was anything like a typical New Town parent he was not convinced that either of them resembled it. But before he could raise any objection, Hamish and the girls had jumped over the wall. There was a children's slide and, as Belinda and Jade slid down it, Hamish led Nigel down a dusty path by the side.

'Now, while the girls are playing we'll try to look as if we are just having a quiet wander around.'

As Hamish suggested, they rambled slowly around the playground taking in the various angles and geography of the place and looking out for suitable vantage points to view the whole. Eventually, they came to the far corner where there was an old rotting sandstone wall and, between two large buttresses, a stone wall with the entrance to a large tunnel. Most of the tunnel was bricked up, but part of it was contained by an iron grille, and there was a padlocked gate.

'There are various places that a package could be concealed here, but this seems to me the most likely. It's the entrance to the old railway tunnel that took the steam trains underground up to Waverley Station. It hasn't been used for many years.'

'Hamish, there's a good chance you're right!' said Nigel. 'In my experience drug gangs have used places like this before. They want to pass the merchandise over but they don't want to meet face to face, and certainly not in a public place!'

'Well,' Hamish said, 'I think you had better get back to your telephone and arrange some serious surveillance for midnight tonight! However, for my part, I'll take the girls up to the beer garden at the Cumberland Bar where they can have their ice cream and I can treat myself to a small refreshment!'

ET IN ARCADIA EGO

Hamish McDavitt had been dining with his great aunt Effie in the Witchery, under the shadow of the castle.

Hamish's parents had died when he was fifteen and sixteen respectively. His father, Hamish senior, suddenly, of a heart attack whilst carving a joint of Aberdeen Angus beef in his butcher's shop in Anstruther. His mother, Ina, who had suffered from a weak heart since contracting rheumatic fever in her youth, died less than a year later. Whilst he was still at school, Hamish had then resided with his aunt and uncle. His father's brother Cecil, pronounced 'See-Sull', had been a fisherman and Hamish loved his tales of the sea and seamen. Some years ago, however, he had died of lung cancer, probably the result of the pipes of thick black shag he always smoked. His aunt Wilhelmina had also passed away, only a few years previously. As his aunt and uncle had no children there were now no McDavitts left in Anstruther and Wilhelmina's mother was the only family that Hamish had.

Euphemia McBean made her way from her home in Kingskettle once a year to see her great-nephew. This was always portrayed as a great chore to her and she would spend a good deal of time lauding the benefits of rural Fife as compared to Edinburgh which, as far as she was concerned, was the devil's drawing room, full of corruption and darkness of the soul.

After Hamish had weaned her from this topic, she would embark on the marginally more interesting subject of the McBean family of generations past. Of Hamish's coming and goings she showed no interest whatsoever. If she was aware that Hamish was now retired from his career as an archivist, there was no indication. Nor indeed was there any indication that she was aware that he was not simply a university student new to the city—as he had been many years ago in 1957.

Hamish generally endured all this with a generous good humour. There was compensation in the fact the Witchery was a superlative restaurant with its dark stone walls, candles and lanterns, pristine white table clothes and red leather seats. Set on a site where, in the dark days, real-life witches or warlocks were harried, tortured and executed, there were also reminders of a gory past in waxen pictures of gaudy enchantresses dancing with the devil.

They dined on hen pheasant with sherry glared parsnips and tournedos of Aberdeen Angus beef with globe artichokes. Aunt Effie had her usual sweet sherry and Hamish, perhaps seeking a little lightness among the heaviness of the evening, eschewed his usual rosy aged Macallan for a younger Bruichladdich, the least peaty of the Islay malts, unusually matured in a Calvados cask. It tripped lightly on the tongue with echoes of newly-mown grass and old school books.

'Ah,' said Hamish, 'Barnacle-bottomed boats on a whale-stranded shore. Seal song and spinning wheels and grannies keening ancient celtic laments on a wind-swept Hebridean beach… '

'Nonsense', said Aunt Effie.

It was an excellent repast at a leisurely pace. However, when Hamish eventually saw his great-aunt on a taxi to the bus station, he felt a little weary. It had been a comparatively long evening with some discussion of deceased relatives that had seemed to get mixed with memories of his own parents. Auntie Effie, he thought, was increasingly losing touch with the real world and sinking into a pastiche of the past. Hamish very much hoped that this was not a fate in store for him in his old age. So, on this particular night he made his way up Castle Hill breathing in the warmish evening air with some relief.

After a couple of minutes, however, he came across his old friend, Edwin McAleese, at the entrance to the Black Swan public house. He was looking from left to right in an agitated kind of way. He saw Hamish coming towards him.

'Hamish, Hamish', he said, 'have you seen Freddie McMaster?'

Hamish knew Freddie, a piper who played in the summer for tourists around the city. 'No. Should I have?'

'Come in, come in and I'll show you.'

They entered the Black Swan and approached a stool at the bar where Edwin was sitting with a large Purser's rum and blackcurrant. Beside it was a half of Bells and a half pint, unfinished, and beside it a pipe and a pouch of tobacco.

'We were sitting here having a dram. Freddie had made a good few bawbees on the Mound, it being such a fine day and all. But he was getting a bit morose. You know, it's the Celtic spirit—I suppose I feel the same myself sometimes. He was moaning about not achieving enough and never having found himself a wife. Said he would be as well throwing himself off the Dean Bridge.' Edwin paused to gulp back the rest of his

40

rum. Then he went to the lavatory and never came back. I've looked all around for him!'

Hamish nodded sagely. 'I see.' He knew that McMaster was subject to these dark humours and that it was not at all the first time he had threatened to throw himself off the Dean Bridge or another of the various bridges and edifices in Edinburgh city centre.

'Do you think he really has gone to throw himself off the bridge. Should we call the police?'

'I think that may be a bit premature,' suggested Hamish. 'It is a good deal more likely that some other appointment has come to his mind. Tell me, apart from all the gloom and doom, did he mention anything else that seemed unusual tonight.'

'Not really,' Edwin mused. 'Except that he was in a poetic frame of mind. He was quoting from Robert Fergusson's Auld Reekie. He started with the very beginning:

'Auld Reekie, wale o' ilka town
That Scotland kens beneath the moon!
Whare couthy chiels at e'ening meet
Their bizzin craigs and mou' to weet... '

'He was quite sentimental. A little tear came into his eye and he said that Edinburgh was the greatest of all the towns on earth and the only place that a civilised man like himself, a scion of the Gaeltacht, could properly live. But then he carried on and quoted another verse:

'Now stair-head critics, senseless fools,
Censure their aim, and pride their rules,

41

In Luckenbooths wi' glouring e'e,
Their neighbours sma'est fauts descry... '

'In fact, that's when he started getting het up. 'It's a shame, 'he said, 'that such a city should be home to so many petty-minded tyrants, cunning craturs from the Canny Man's, spivs, creeping Jesuses and hypocritical arseholes—the devilish spawn of Calvinism, that sombre intoxication that is death unto our hearts, as the big man said!' And he became quite imated for a time. Then, after another couple of halves, he grew morose, and then he disappeared.'

'Well,' said Hamish, 'remember that Freddie is a son of the manse. Sounds like quite typical behaviour to me. Some people would call it the Caledonian antisyzygy!'

'Hmm,' said Edwin, not inclined to get into a discussion of an obscure piece of Scottish literary theory about the reconciliation of opposites, ' ...But the fact is that he has disappeared, and the waste of a good dram!' After a pause he added, 'Perhaps we should finish it—so it won't go to waste, of course. And then maybe we could have a wee look for him.'

'Excellent idea,' said Hamish, grateful for a little adventure after the tedium of the evening, 'We'll check out some of his other haunts. And since we are in a poetic frame of mind, let's try the Forresthill Bar first. It's up by the Bedlam where Robert Fergusson came to an untimely end at the tender age of twenty-four. Poor soul. Burns remembered him and paid for a monument down by the Canongate Kirk. There's a statue of Fergusson outside of it now.'

They walked up Fleshmarket Close and up past St Giles, taking a slightly more circuitous route in the hope that they might come across the lost piper, but when they came to George IV Bridge they were confronted by a police cordon and an assembly of fire engines.

'Oh, my God,' said Edwin, 'It must be him!'

'Hold on,' said Hamish. He approached a weary-looking police officer.

'Good evening, sergeant,' he said, recognising his rank, 'Is it a jumper?'

' 'Fraid so,' said the police sergeant, 'clogging up the system just when we had six tourist buses heading down to King's Stables Road.'

'Is it by any chance an elderly man with a beard in full Highland dress?'

'Goodness me, no. It's a young Australian backpacker, stuck up on the parapet pissed as a fart. With a bit of luck we'll have him down in a mo and let you through.'

'There we are,' said Hamish. 'Nothing to worry about at all, just a drunken caper.' They were at David Hume's statue opposite St Giles. The great philosopher was sitting rather incongruously in a sort of Roman toga, his flesh smooth in a greeny bronze. Little knots of people were milling around. Not just tourists but also students out for a night on the town, punters from Leith full of Friday night whiskies, couples dressed for the concert hall or a dinner party in the Grange or the New Town. All of the humanity that Edinburgh had to offer was, it seemed, abroad that night.

'Some nights,' Hamish said. 'seem to be something out of the ordinary, as if they have a special flavour or significance that will live in the memory. I'm reminded of the words of a famous Edinburgh poet.'

'What,' you mean Fergusson?' suggested Edwin.

'No, no. I'm thinking of a more recent poet, Sydney Goodsir Smith. He imagined a sort of mythological Edinburgh, where legend mixed with the everyday happenings of folk.'

He thought for a moment then he quoted a few lines:

'And trulie there are maitters o' great moment
Abraid the day—
As the great michtie
In their great seats are warslan
For another cushion maybe,
Or mair licht
Or the table
A wee thing nearer til the great hand…'

'Don't think I've heard that one,' said Edwin.

'It's from a poem called *Under the Eildon Tree*. The Eildon Tree in myth was a tree with magical powers. The medieval Scottish post, Thomas the Rhymer, fell asleep under its boughs and was transported to Fairyland.'

'Well, *that's* OK,' said Edwin, 'but who cares about the great and the good. That's what Freddie was raging about, wasn't it. Isn't it the ordinary folk of Edinburgh that matter to us?'

Hamish laughed. 'You're right, Edwin,' he said. 'I was getting a little carried away. Goodsir Smith came from the landed classes himself. But he had the common touch too. In one poem he imagines all the historical figures of old Edinburgh: Burns's Clarinda, Queen Mary in her bathtub, the 'Electric Shepherd'—also known as James Hogg—Deacon Brodie, Fergusson himself, all mixing at the World's End in the High Street with the folk of the 'rortie wretched city'. It's in a poem called *Kynd Kittock's Land*, after Kynd Kittock, who was the keeper of a fine shebeen in the Old Town. I can recite you a verse of it:

'The rortie wretched city
Sair come doun frae its auld hiechts
—The hauf o't smug, complacent,
Lost til all pride of race or spirit,
The tither wild and rouch as ever
In its secret hairt… '

By this time they had come to the Forresthill Bar, and it was wild and rouch indeed, with chattering drinkers spilling out the door and from the back corner, the frantic sound of a session in full swing. The plaintive tones of *Leaving Lismore* were followed by a more lively rendition of *The Reel of Tullochgorum*. Fiddlers' elbows thrashing to and fro, tin whistles whistling. There was an elderly woman energetically bashing a bodhran and, in the centre, a little old man playing a guitar with unbelievable dexterity, shaping, it seemed, a different chord for each note of the melody. 'Peerie Willie's in fine form tonight,' said Edwin.

They struggled to the bar and Hamish insisted that Edwin have a 'malt of the moment', a twelve-year-old Tomatin. 'We'll drink to the big man himself, Seumas Mor, whose bust is above the bar with a bottle of Lagavulin. He was a great poet of Edinburgh and he portrayed it as a place where good and bad, life and death were in continual conflict.' He recited a verse:

'Floret silva undique
We'll hae a ball, though the Deil's to pay.

The quick and the slaw are game for a tear,
Sma'back snooves from his Greyfriars lair.
Out of the darkness the queer coves come,
Janus guisers from bield and tomb:
Scrunchit hurdies and raw-bone heid
Junkies mell wi' the livin deid.
Get stuck in Hornie, and show's the way.
The lily, the rose, the rose I lay.'

In the end, they had a pleasing interlude at the Forresthill Bar, known to all the locals as Sandy Bell's after an earlier landlord. But Charlie Hog—the landlord of the present day —had not seen Freddie McMaster that day or for some time previously.

After they had visited the Bow Bar without success, Edwin said, 'Let's try the Heb. Maybe that's where we should have gone first. He's often in there after he's been busking on the Mound.'

The Hebrides was a small pub behind the railway station that was known to be frequented by Highlanders and where, quite often, despite the confined nature of the premises, a piper would blow up a reel or a pibroch, often to the astonishment of passing tourists. Tonight, the pub was quite busy, although there was no sign of a single piper. Brian, the bar manager, confirmed that Freddie McMaster had not been seen that day. They had a Lagavullin and a rum for Edwin. In the corner, a small Chinese-looking man with a tartan tammy was strumming a guitar and singing folk songs. He was accompanied on the banjo by a tall blind man with a long white beard and a shaggy dog at his feet. A chorus reverberated in the smoky fug of the bar:

'With my roving eye,
Fal de diddle die,
Rolling eye dum derry,
With my roving eye.'

At the back of the bar, three German tourists were unfolding a street plan of the city. Edwin was gazing towards the window seat where two attractive young women, possibly sisters, were sipping pints of Guinness and smoking Gauloise cigarettes. They had black hair and red lipsticked lips and were uniformly dressed in black striped Breton tops. However, when a snatch of their conversation drifted bar, it had a distinct West Lothian rather than a Gallic tilt.

'Aren't those lassies braw?' asked Edwin.

Hamish looked down across the bar. 'I think you're right, he said. The great Edinburgh poets always had an eye for a bonny lassie. There was Stella Cartwright, the muse of Rose Street, and there was… ' Hamish hesitated, suddenly becoming aware that they were, by now, both suffering a little from the effect of several drams.

A moment later, two large hands placed themselves on both their shoulders. 'Good evening, gentlemen.' It was the blind banjo player. 'I recognised you both from your fine lilting lowland voices! What are you getting yourselves up to tonight?'

'Well, Bill, originally we were looking for Freddie McMaster, the piper,' said Hamish, 'but now Edwin is eyeing up some lassies from Bathgate and, in the meantime, we've been discussing the poetry of Sydney Goodsir Smith underneath the statue of David Hume.'

'Ah, Sydney Goodsir Smith,' he said, 'I know him. A bit of a lad. He was always finding whores and idolising them as if they were Venus or Aphrodite. I remember a verse':

'I got her i' the Black Bull
(The Black Bull o' Norroway)
Gin I mynd richt, in Leith Street,
Doun the stair at the corner forenent
The Fun Fair and Museum of Monstrosities... '

'Reminds me of this place a bit!' interjected Edwin.

'Ah, well, maybe. But the Black Bull, That's the Black Bull at top of Leith Walk,' said Edwin. 'It's an old old place. They say that Burns used to drink there when he was staying in the White Hart in the Grassmarket. It's all just young people and the rock music now.'

'Funnily enough, there's also a Black Bull in the Grassmarket now, just beside the White Hart,' noted Hamish.

'And I'll tell you,' added Bill, a few years ago there was one at the bottom of Leith Walk too. It was owned by the same pub company and it was done up in exactly the same way. Now, I'll tell you an interesting story about those pubs. One day an old friend of mine, wee Johnnie from Wick, was in the pub on his way home. And after a few jars he called for a taxi to take him home to Dalkeith. After a while when the taxi didn't turn up he phoned them again. The taxi said the taxi was right outside the door waiting for him and the driver was inside looking for him. 'That's not right,' said Johnnie, looking all around. Then he went to the door and realised what was wrong. With the pubs being the same and all, he thought that he was in the Black Bull in the Grassmarket, when in fact, he was in the Black Bull in Leith Walk!'

Hamish had been listening intently to this little story when suddenly a distant look came into his eyes and he screwed up his face a little. 'Excuse us, Bill,' he said, 'I've just thought of something! Finish your rum, Edwin. I just want to check something around the corner.'

They walked up a narrow dark close into Victoria Street.

'Et in arcadia ego,' said Hamish suddenly.

'What?' asked Edwin.

'Oh, they are words from an inscription on a painting by Nicolas Poussin—you may have seen his work in the National Gallery on the Mound—but it is used by another well-known Scottish poet—Ian Hamilton Finlay. You'll see it inscribed in his sculpture garden down at Little Sparta in Lanarkshire'

'And what does it mean?'

'Well, nobody is quite sure, but it's something like, 'here in Arcadia, I will reside', and it reminded me of where we are going now.'

They had been walking up Victoria Street and now, right enough, on the right hand side, they came to the Arcade Bar!

'It just occurred to me,' said Hamish, 'Edinburgh is a city of ups and downs. 'Precipitous City' it has been called. Here we are in the Arcade Bar in Victoria Street but directly above us is where we started off, the Black Swan in the High Street! They were just one hotel at one time.'

They entered the bar and Hamish ordered the usual from the barman. When he received his change he asked, 'You haven't by any chance had a customer tonight, a bearded man in full highland dress?'

The barman rolled his eyes in a gesture of exasperation. 'I have indeed. He just came in our of nowhere and he says that

49

he had a half and a half and his pipe and baccy pouch on the bar. 'Someone must have stolen it,' he says. I say nonsense and he gets quite bolshy. Upsetting the customers he was so I had to ask him to leave. He wasn't awful happy about it, 'I'm telling you,' he says, 'I'm gaun hame to bed noo, but I'll be back in the morn to see the manager And that was that.'

Hamish chuckled. 'It's quite clear now what has happened. Freddie went to the lavatory, which is downstairs from the Black Swan, but instead of going back upstairs, he took the other staircase and came down here. He was so puggled with the drink that he didn't recognise that he was in another bar!'

Hamish was right and Freddie McMaster was safe in bed at home, not rotting in the Dene under the Dean Bridge. Hamish and Edwin had had quite an entertaining night and they concluded it with another dram and some words fiom another poetic son of Scotland:

'Beautiful city of Edinburgh!
Where the tourist can drown his sorrow
By viewing your monuments and statues fine
During the lovely summer time
I'm sure it will his spirits cheer
As Sir Walter Scott's monument he draws near,
That stands in East Prince's Street
Amongst flowery gandens, fine and neat.'

Hamish said, 'It's been a grand night. We've solved a mystery and had a poetic excursion and seen a bit of the two sides of Edinburgh—the light and the dark, the old and the new, the sacred and the profane.' And on that heady thought, they both decided that it was time to retire to their beds themselves.

THE FAIRY CUP OF DUN ACAINN

It was a cold February day with freezing rain turning to sleet when Hamish McDavitt walked down Victoria Street—past Ron's Old Town bookshop with its display of Shepherd and Swarbreck prints of old Edinburgh and Mellis's cheese shop with its pungent aromas—to meet his friend, Inspector Nigel Stonelaw of the Edinburgh and Lothians Police, in the Bow Bar.

The Bow Bar was a fine old Edinburgh establishment, its walls covered in old mirrors and advertisements—Melvin & Co Pale Ale; Studio Cigarettes; Sheriff's Jamaica Rum; Thomson and Porteous Half Dark Nailrod.

Today, Hamish found Stonelaw unusually ruffled. After purchasing a couple of malt whiskies, McDavitt asked him if he was having any difficulties at work.

'Well...' Stonelaw started, frowning a little. 'It"s a rum case, Hamish. And I don't mind admitting it has left me looking a right fool, and all over something that rightfully should have nothing to do with us at all. Have you heard of the Fairy Cup of Dun Acainn?'

Hamish thought for a moment. 'It sounds familiar—but you had better explain.'

'It's a quaich, a two handled drinking cup, but a very special one indeed. Here, maybe this will explain.' He handed McDavitt a cutting from the *Scots Magazine*.

'The Fairy Cup of Dun Acainn,' McDavitt read, 'has a very curious history indeed. Its story is first recounted in Kirk's *The Secret Commonwealth*, and it is a story that bears some remarkable resemblances to other stories of fairy enchantment, including the fabulous tale of Thomas the Rhymer.' Hamish paused to scan some illustrations: prints from an illustrated edition of Andrew Lang's *Fairy Books* and an old plate of Thomas of Ercildoune seated under the enchanted eildon tree. He continued reading: 'The story goes that, many years ago, Aonghas MacFhionghuin, the family piper of the McKinnon family, became insanely jealous of Dòmhnall Ban Mhic Criomain, the hereditary piper of the MacLeods of Skye, whose skill at the pibroch was reputedly due to a enchanted chanter given to him by the queen of the fairies. Aonghas became so weary of his own limited skills that one day he went into a rage and shouted to the fairies to take his life away, as he was not worthy of an instrument that he could control so poorly. Now, the fairy sibh happened to be passing that day and the Fairy Queen took pity on him and brought him into the Otherworld. And there the best fairy pipers taught Aonghas how to play the pipes. For seven years he learned, and for another seven he practised, and for a final seven he was allowed to play the pipes for the Fairy Queen alone who was well satisfied with him. And at the end of the final seven years, the Fairy Queen said 'Aonghas, you have served me well, and now you can return to the world of men.' But before he departed, she presented him with an enchanted quaich, promising him that, if ever he himself, or any other McKinnon, felt that they had lost their talent for the great music, they should drink from the Fairy Cup and it would be restored. The quaich, known as the Fairy Cup of Dun Acainn after the McKinnon stronghold on Skye, has remained in the family for generations and is now in the possession of the brothers Hector and Alastair McKinnon, who have vowed to restore the McKinnon ancestral home to its original glory.'

McDavitt looked up his reading and restored his little folding reading glasses to their case. 'I take it, then, Nigel, that something has happened to the fabled cup?'

Stonelaw nodded glumly. 'Well, let me tell you the whole sorry tale. Apparently, some weeks ago the McKinnons received a couple of anonymous letters suggesting that someone was intending to steal the Cup. Subsequently, they took precautions. They increased the insurance, they installed new security devices and, most tellingly of all, they employed a security adviser, Fraser McLean, a retired detective sergeant from the Highlands and Islands Constabulary, to take charge of security at the castle. But the McKinnons, apparently, are acquainted with Chief Superintendent Ord, my immediate superior. He promised to send his best officer to give the place the once over.'

McDavitt chuckled. 'I presume that that was yourself?'

'Well, yes. And not unsurprising considering the successful apprehension of the Scotland Yard heroin traffickers—and, besides, Inspector Rubrik was otherwise engaged.'

McDavitt knew that Stonelaw sometimes had a good conceit of himself and had probably failed to remember the part that Hamish himself had played in the Scotland Yard case.

'So yo took a little trip to the ancestral home of the no. McKinnons, off the coast of Skye.'

'Yes, and a right stormy day it was. The rain was raining that horizontal way that it does sometimes in Scotland. We drove up through Glencoe where the mountains seem to be ready to topple right over you, then up through the Great Glen where the rain turned to sleet and then snow, and over the bridge at Kyle to where the castle stood on a small island just off the coast. When we got to the jetty we were very reluctant to go over to the castle at all in the little motor launch they provided. But we were assured it was safe. It's not an experience I would like to repeat, you know, the sea as black with whipped up little peaks of foam and the boat pitched back and forward and rolled from side to side.'

Hamish nodded, 'I know what you mean. Although my ancestors were seafarers themselves, I'm wary of the sea.'

'Yes,' said Stonelaw I remember you told me what Dr Johnson said—that being in a boat is like being in jail with the additional risk of drowning!

Stonelaw continued: 'The castle itself was a little dark and austere, with a good part of it still in scaffolding, but the grand hall itself was welcoming if a little draughty, with a great roaring log fire and a good brandy from a crystal decanter. The brothers McKinnon seemed decent enough sorts. Ord had told me a little about them. Alastair, the younger, had trained as an accountant. He was a projects man, behind the planning of the resurrected Castle Moil. A stickler for detail almost to the point of pedantry. He seemed seriously concerned about the preservation of the Fairy Cup. Hector was a more jovial sort. He was much more involved in the community, raising petitions against the proposed wind farms, taking part in the Camanachd Club, community drama and all that sort of stuff.

'They both apologised for what might have been perceived as a lack of hospitality, but Hector explained that building work had been suspended because of the poor weather and that the building was only occupied by themselves, a housekeeper, and Fraser McLean, who was currently inspecting the perimeter for any security lapses. Then Hector took my detective constable and the boatsman down to the kitchens to arrange some lunch and to dry off our overcoats. Meanwhile, Alastair took me up to the library to see the Fairy Cup.

'The Cup was kept in a display case against one wall of the library, surrounded by book shelves with a variety of volumes, mostly on clan and family history, but with some dog-eared old Penguins and Pelicans as well. The case was made of solid oak and reinforced glass and protected by double locks and an alarm. I can't say that the Cup itself impressed me enormously. It was a large piece of slightly misshapen and tarnished beaten silver with bulky horn handles encrusted with uneven and quite gaudy gemstones.

'Anyway, while Alastair McKinnon was explaining some of the history of the Cup and the clan McKinnon, the door swung open and Fraser McLean entered. He was dressed in a Barbour jacket, green Wellington boots and a tartan tammy. He was dripping from the wet and carrying a clipboard covered with polythene. A broad-shouldered type with a ruddy face and a full head of hair, moustache and sideburns that were partly ginger but turning grey. He coughed and wheezed a little and had to take a breath from a puffer to settle himself.

'We made our introductions and McLean apologised for his delayed appearance. He had, he said, just wanted to do a final check on the entrances before we came in order to avoid any discrepancies. Alastair McKinnon left us to have our talk and we settled into two large leather armchairs by the bay windows overlooking the peaks and troughs of the stormy sea, I must say, I took to Fraser McLean at once—a bluff straightforward man respectful of his position and keen to do his job thoroughly and well. We went over the security arrangements and I have to say he seemed to have thought of more or less everything, but still he was keen to solicit my advice and took numerous notes on the margins of his clipboard.

'After a while, Hector McKinnon came into the library. He seemed delighted to see that McLean and I were getting on so well. Some lunch had been prepared for us but first he wanted to let me have a closer look at the Cup itself. He beckoned to McLean, who took a bulky set of keys from his pocket and opened the cabinet. He also took out a bottle of malt and poured a little into the cup and sipped it. 'Please examine the cup', he said, handing it to me. I held the Fairy Cup in my hand for a moment. It seemed lighter than I had expected and the gems glowed in a peculiar way. 'I would personally be delighted to serve you a dram from the Cup, Inspector, but tradition has it that if aught but a McKinnon sups from the Fairy Cup he will be spirited away to Tir-nan-Og, the land of dreams, and never return.' He took another sip and held out the Cup. ' …But, of course, I thought better of it, drink and duty never mix.

'Hector and I went down to lunch and left McLean to lock away the Cup and complete his notes. We had venison and blackcurrant jelly sandwiches with mugs of hot milky tea and were generally quite relaxed when Hector remembered McLean. 'He can be a bit fastidious, you know. I'll go and fetch him.'

'But merely a minute or so later, we heard a cry from the direction of the library and, to cut a long story short, when we arrived the Fairy Cup was gone and so was McLean. Alastair shook his head in disbelief and then turned to his brother: 'I told you so, I told you so…'

'It turned out, in fact, that the McLeans were the old clan rivals of the McKinnons. Alastair had wanted to thwart Fraser McLean's appointment for that reason, but Hector had poo-pooed the idea, calling it old-fashioned nonsense.

'However, whatever the cause, the fact is that when the police arrived from Portree, then reinforcements from Inverness, Fraser McLean was not to be found and neither was the Cup. We checked everything, My own detective constable was in the kitchen overlooking the jetty all the time of our visit and the motor launch had not been used. It was impossible that anyone could have swum to the shore and survived in the conditions. There was no other way off the island. Amazingly, Fraser McLean had vanished into thin air, perhaps as the fairies had predicted! And when we checked his references, unfortunately, we found it wasn't the real sergeant McLean at all, who had retired to raise long-haired, black-faced sheep on Barra, but an impostor.'

'And that's it, Hamish, You can imagine our colleagues from the Highlands and Islands Constabulary had a bloody good laugh at our expense. A precious antique spirited away under our very noses. I don't know when I'll stop having nightmares about the whole thing.'

McDavitt laughed. 'Don't despair, Nigel, maybe we can rescue you from these troubled nights.' He took a long sip of his whisky.

'Now, I only have one little question. Answer it in as simple a way as you can: the two brothers, Hector and Alastair, are they similar in appearance?'

'They are both balding and slim, and they dress similarly

in tartan trews and a short-cut jacket. But otherwise they are quite distinct. Hector is slightly taller, wears horn-rimmed spectacles with bottle-bottom lens and talks in a quite high-pitched excitable sort of way while Alastair is a slower, more deliberate type.'

'Excellent. Well, I think I can resolve this problem for you.'

'What, already!'

Hamish smiled. 'It's really quite a simple little conundrum, Nigel. Let me take a minute to explain. Now, here for example, are the two malt whiskies we bought a moment ago-Glenfiddich and Glenmorangie. Both popular but perfectly adequate Speyside malts, quite similar in tone and texture. Please take a sniff and a slow sip of both.'

Stonelaw nosed the malts as he had been shown by McDavitt, and sipped both, taking a moment to feel the taste saturate his tongue.

McDavitt continued, 'The Glenfiddich is slightly fruity and dry, with a finish of slightly overripe bananas. The Glenmorangie, on the other hand, is similar, but a little more exotic, reminiscent of apricots or dates, perhaps stewed in a mild curry sauce, with an overtone of citrus fruits' Hamish took a sip himself. 'That's why, if you come across a sassenach who doesn't know how to pronounce Glenmorangie, you tell them that it's 'orangey'.'

'Yes,' said Stonelaw, 'I think I see what you mean, now that you explain it that way'

'We can all learn the art of taste and subtle discrimination, but it doesn't come naturally. In fact, life throws so many tastes and experiences at us that it is all to easy to lump them together with misconceptions.

'For example, take a sister drink to whisky, vodka.

I don't care for it myself, but if you go the Polish club in Drummond Place you will find my friend Marek, who is a great connoisseur of its different varieties. And yet, let me surprise you. Although we all know the difference between whisky and vodka—one is amber, the other clear, one served at room temperature, the other chilled, etcetera—in different conditions our discrimination is limited!

'Take a dozen people, blindfold them and, without any further information, give them a little whisky and vodka in a plastic container and you will find that less than fifty percent of them will tell the difference!'

Stonelaw had followed this discourse carefully but was now a little perplexed. 'That's all very well, Hamish, but what has it to do with the McKinnon case?'

'Well, it too was a matter of discrimination. I asked you if the McKinnon brothers were similar and you told me what I wanted to know, but it was the opposite of what you thought you had told me! You concluded that they were quite different, but what you told me was that they were very similar. Slim, bald—making it easier to wear a wig, by the way—dressed in more or less identical clothes. On the other hand, the differences—thick spectacles, a squeaky voice, a little more height (with the aid of heels) could all be assumed quite easily by a skilled performer.

'Only at your entrance and departure did you see the McKinnon brothers together. Otherwise, I suspect that Alastair managed to play both the parts of his brother and himself. Hector, with his experience of amateur dramatics, took on the slightly tougher role, that of Fraser McLean, with the wig and facial hair, the asthmatic wheeze to disguise his own distinctive voice and the padded Barbour jacket to bulk out his own slight frame. Hector must have been delighted that you took to him so readily. It was easy for McLean to disappear as he never existed in the first place!'

Stonelaw's jaw dropped as he contemplated Hamish's revelation. 'Good God, Hamish, now that I think about it I'm sure that you're right. There was something not quite right about McLean—and we never noticed!'

'Don't concern yourself. We often fail to notice what is in front of our nose, wasn't it the good Dr Doyle who coined the phrase: 'there are many things that are obvious that are never, by any chance, observed.''

'But what has happened to the Fairy Cup?'

'Oh, I wouldn't worry about that. The McKinnons will have it in safe keeping. Apart from the curse, they couldn't bear to part with it. After all, they have owned it for five hundred years.' He paused and took on a slightly more serious tone. 'On the other hand, they probably thought that the insurance money would go a long way to realising their dream of resurrecting Castle Moil.'

'They won't be doing much of that now when the Fraud Squad catches up with them!'

Stonelaw was quite splenetic, and Hamish put a calming hand on his shoulder. 'Well, Nigel, perhaps we shouldn't be so hasty. It was a very ingenious plot and impressively carried out. Hector carried off his part wonderfully and fooled you completely. And, of course, that nonsense about Tir nan Og, a delightful touch!'

The Inspector's brows were furrowed, and a dark complexion came over his face.

'Ahem... Well, of course, there's no real need to mention all that. Here's what I suggest: why don't you have a quiet word with them, over a wee dram? Suppose the cup were to suddenly reappear, perhaps washed ashore with the remains of an old Barbour jacket. The insurers would be mollified, your own reputation restored, and the resulting media coverage itself might raise a pretty penny for the restoration of the castle.

'Besides, it would be good to see the Fairy Cup of Dun Acainn restored to its rightful place. One of these days I might have a sip of uisque beatha, the elixir of life, from it myself. But meantime, I'll content myself to sit here and have another dram.'

THE CASE OF THE WRONG NECKLACE

Hamish McDavitt was sitting in the Canongate Century Club in Carrubers Close with Robert Ord, Chief Superintendent of the Edinburgh and Lothian Police. They were discussing issues of mutual interest such as Ord's recent serialisation of the infamous Gilchrist murder case in the *Daily Scot* and the latest sensational Edinburgh crime, the murder of Lady Dalhousie in her house in the Grange—apparently the result of a botched robbery.

'I'm afraid we haven't made much real progress at all,' said Ord. 'It's disappointing and a bit embarrassing considering the high profile of the victim.' Ord shrugged. 'I suppose you're familiar with the case, Hamish?'

'Well, only what I've read in the newspapers.'

Ord shrugged. 'Well, there isn't a lot more I can tell you than that. At first it seemed a fairly conventional if unpleasant crime. At around 3.00am on the morning of the twenty-sixth of April, a person unknown broke into the Dalhousie family home in the Grange. It was a professional job. A wall had been scaled, the alarm short-circuited and entrance effected through the French windows. As the burglar was emptying the safe, it seems, he was disturbed by Lady Dalhousie. She was clubbed over the head with a jemmy—the murder weapon was found lying in situ, unfortunately without any fingerprints— and died instantly. The burglar had then flown but, strangely, all of the jewels from the safe, with one exception, were found abandoned at the bottom of the garden.'

'What was the exceptional item?'

'A diamond necklace. Victorian. A family heirloom of some value.'

'And the intruder escaped without interference?'

'Not quite. After he had scaled the wall in some haste, he bumped into a Mr James Chalmers, a war veteran returning late from a veteran's dinner.'

'Did Mr Chalmers get a good view of him then?'

'Seemingly, but unfortunately Mr Chalmers has a condition that is due to shell shock at the end of the last war. It means that he can see well enough to get by but he has difficulty in focusing or recognising specific features. All he could tell us is that the intruder appeared to be a male of medium height.'

'Hmm. That's not very helpful.' Hamish took a sip of his whisky, a Jura with a slightly peated pungency reminiscent of tacketty boots sinking into the damp turf of a seldom-visited hillside. 'So how did you proceed with the case?'

'In actual fact it seemed straightforward at first. There are only a few burglars in Edinburgh who would attempt such a thing. Cat burglars, they're called. Willing to enter premises that are occupied. They tend to be smarter than the average burglar, researching and targeting a specific victim—not at all the sort that kicks in a door in Muirhouse to get money for drugs.'

'So we got the CID on the case and tried to match our records with the modus operandi of the crime. It came up with just four matches—all well known to us: Frankie Manson, Bert McAuley, Freddie Ferguson and Chic Millar.'

'I presume you followed up on all these suspects.'

'Oh yes, it didn't take long. Bert McAuley, as it turned out, was already keeping her Majesty company, in Peterhead, for his involvement in a credit card scam, and Freddie Ferguson was laid up with a broken leg, supposedly from falling off his bicycle—although we had our suspicions about that. We made some progress when we visited Chic Millar. He seemed to have come into some money—the house was full of drink and packaging that seemed to be for a newly purchased home cinema. But Chic had an unassailable alibi—he was in Preston at his niece's wedding on the day in question. Besides, the whole thing seemed out of character for Chic. He was a bit more of an opportunist thief, known as 'the prowler' for his tendency to lurk about unnoticed awaiting an opportunity.'

'Only one suspect left then!'

'Yes, and we thought we'd cracked it when we discovered that a gentleman of Frankie's description, but with a newly formed growth of beard, was reported pawning a diamond necklace at one of the city's more respectable pawnbrokers.'

'And was it the stolen necklace?'

'Unfortunately not. The necklace was hot, but it was from another robbery entirely. Stolen from an old lady in Corstorphine who had foolishly left her door open when she went shopping. We found Frankie and he confessed to stealing it and is currently on remand in Saughton. He'll probably get two to three years.'

'So all your prime suspects were exhausted.'

'We were disappointed, it's true. But then we had to consider other possibilities. It did seem strange that only one item was actually stolen—that didn't seem typical of many conventional burglars. Perhaps the necklace had some particular significance that we didn't understand? And then.

of course, there was the possibility that the burglary was just a cover-up for the murder of Lady Dalhousie.'

'That is always a possibility, and there could be a variety of reasons.'

Hamish looked thoughtful. 'I suppose you have interviewed the family?'

'We're just at the stage of doing that, Obviously the murder and the funeral has been a terrible shock for the Dalhousie family, and Lord Dalhousie is a very important person in Edinburgh society. It's a tricky ease that has to be handled with both urgency and delicacy We've put our best man, Inspector Rubrik, on to it.'

The lights faded slightly. A discreet sign that the club would soon be emptying for the evening

'Any ideas, Hamish?'

Hamish paused for a moment. 'Nothing that I can think of.' He shrugged. 'You're right, there isn't very much to go on. I suspect that a great deal more evidence will have to be amassed before any conclusions can be drawn.' The lights flickered on and off twice and Hamish rose to get his coat.

'In the circumstances, I can only wish Inspector Rubrik good fortune with this case.'

Ord wrapped himself in his voluminous overcoat and took his old pipe from his pocket.

'Well, good night, Hamish.' He added, 'I'll let you know if anything turns up in the Dalhousie case.'

Some two weeks later, Hamish was taking advantage of an unseasonably warm Spring day and strolling through Princes Street Gardens beneath the battlements of Edinburgh Castle, when he came across Ord, sitting on a park bench puffing on his pipe and musing over a crossword puzzle. He sat down beside him.

'Day off, Bob?'

'Ach, Hamish! Unfortunately not; just a lunch hour, escaping from the trials at the office. I often sit here. Edinburgh may be a village, but it is also such an anonymous city that you can sit in the middle of it and no-one bothers you at all.'

Hamish glanced down at the crossword puzzle which was about half completed. 'Who is it today?'

'It's Rebus. Always an awkward wee bugger!' Ord was referring to the crossword compiler, one of a series of coded names that varied from day to day. 'Can't get 3 down at all.'

Hamish looked at the clue for 3 down. It read 'Young thief not serving time (15).'

They sat in silence for a little while, appreciating the warm sun, until, suddenly, they were awakened from their reverie by the sound of the one o'clock gun sounding from the battlements of the castle.

'I think it's a literary reference.' Hamish said. A quote from Edward Young, who wrote *Night Thoughts*, The answer's 'procrastination', because 'procrastination is the thief of time!'

Ord pencilled in the answer. 'Excellent, Hamish. That makes 10 across 'cardoman' and 4 down could be 'uxoricide''

He continued to add the answers as he took a contented puff of his pipe, then he put down the pencil and newspaper and sighed. 'Wish it were so easy to solve this damned necklace murder.'

'Ah, does that mean you've made no progress with the Dalhousie case, then?'

'Practically none. It is not without difficulty investigating a family of such standing in society. We've uncovered a few skeletons in closets. Lady Dalhousie, it turns out, was addicted to barbiturates. Not too serious, but she wasn't getting about much. Lord Dalhousie had been seen on more than one occasion at Phantasy Island, a sort of dancing and showgirl club on a boat moored off Leith harbour. There had also been some dispute about the necklace when it had been passed down from Dalhousie's mother as to which of her offspring should get it. But these are fairly typical of the sort of things you get when you dig deep. Nothing to make a case out of. Inspector Rubrik is fairly peeved.'

Ord filled his pipe with another handful of deep black shag. 'I fear, Hamish, that we might have another unsolved murder in our files in fifty years time—a bit like the Gilchrist case.'

Hamish suddenly started. He gazed up at the hazy outline of the castle against the sun as if lost in his thoughts.

'What's up, Hamish?' said Ord, looking at him inquisitively. 'Thought of something?

Hamish hesitated for a minute before looking back towards Ord.

'Something just occurred to me. Cat burglars, you said, are smarter than the average criminal. Perhaps they also read newspapers!'

'I don't get you.'

'The burglary was carried out on the twenty-sixth, a Sunday. On the twenty-fifth the first part of your serialisation of the Gilchrist case appeared in the *Daily Scot*. Do you remember what part of the story that covered?'

'Of course. Miss Gilchrist had been murdered and a precious brooch stolen. A German Jew was arrested after he had sold a precious brooch. It turned out to be a different brooch and this formed a crucial part of his defence... '

'Although he was still prosecuted due to the ineptitude of the police!' Hamish interrupted, 'The gentleman in question was the famous Oscar Slater, who had unjustly been prosecuted and served many years in jail before his being released after campaigning by, among others, Sir Arthur Conan Doyle.'

'Well yes,' Ord frowned slightly, 'but he was pardoned at a later date. What are you getting at, Hamish?'

'I think we may have been misled. In a very clever way, but we should have seen through the ruse. I think I know were you might find your murderer. In a very convenient location indeed—Saughton prison!'

'What!' He thought for while, obviously surprised. Then his face lit up. 'Don't tell me! You mean Frankie Manson, don't you?'

'Yes. Suppose Manson had carried out the burglary. It's in keeping with his record. It all goes smoothly but then he is interrupted. It is a shock. Lady Dalhousie is high on her drugs and possibly wanders aimlessly in the dark. Manson gets such a surprise that he hits out. It is not what he intends but he sees that his victim is dead. He knows enough about the law to realise the seriousness of his situation. He could be found guilty of murder and faces a great deal of time behind bars. He panics, drops the jemmy and runs with the loot. Outside he bumps into Mr Chalmers. He continues to run but then he calms down. His profession is nothing if not one that encourages him to think on his feet.'

'Of course, Manson wouldn't know about the old man's sight problem. He would see himself as deeper in trouble, with an eyewitness able to testify to his presence at the murder scene.'

'But Manson is clever And he has read, just the previous

day, your account of the Gilchrist case. This enables him to hatch a plan He returns to the house a little later and throws the remainder of the spoils over the wall, keeping the necklace. Now he knows of a similar necklace. It has been stolen by the opportunist thief, Chic Millar, from a house in Corstorphine a few days previously. He goes to see Millar and buys the necklace. That is why, when your men visit Millar, he has come into some money.'

'I'm beginning to see' Ord intervened, ' …and then he takes the other necklace to the pawnshop, a respectable pawnbroker, unlike the fence he would normally use… and he has a growth of beard. Just in case, thinking he may be recognised if the old man has provided a photo-fit.'

'Paradoxically, he wants to be recognised, but only for having the necklace, for that is the red herring that he hopes will distract attention from the crime!'

Ord shook his head ruefully, but then, seeing the cleverness of the ploy, almost broke out into a little chuckle. 'We didn't think, Hamish. In our haste to book him for the crime he has confessed to, the crime that he didn't commit, we didn't consider any alternatives.'

'No doubt Manson was relieved that you accepted his story What better place for a criminal to hide than in a prison!'

And it turned out, as always, that Hamish McDavitt was right, and, after Chic Millar admitted the sale of the wrong necklace to Frankie Manson, Manson confessed, revealing the hiding place of the original necklace, and accepted a plea of guilty to manslaughter with mitigating circumstances, and Inspector Rubrik, as usual, got most of the credit.

A POTATO RIDDLE

It was the Saturday before Christmas and Hamish McDavitt was browsing in Bert Barrott's bookshop in the West Port. In general terms, Hamish approved of Christmas. He liked the bright lights in Princes Street, the giant Christmas tree on the Mound—an annual gift from the Norwegian government—the skaters in Princes Street Gardens and the German Market, with cheerful stalls selling borsch and bratwursts and cut-out paper models and wooden decorations. Sometimes, however, he thought the whole thing dragged on too long, and today he was glad to get away from the crowds of shoppers and chose some Christmas presents of his own.

Hamish's rather negative opinion of Christmas, however, was nothing as compared to his opinion of the Edinburgh New Year. Once Edinburgh folk had gathered at the Tron on Hogmanay for the bells, then first-footed each other with a wee dram, a lump of coal and a tin of shortbread warmth, food and drink for the rest of the year. But now the city fathers, in their wisdom, had decided to seal off the entire city centre and charge a ridiculous sum for entrance to a street party where mostly young folk and foreigners drank themselves senseless on cheap lager while listening to raucous pop music.

Hamish shuddered at the very thought of it. However, today had been a successful excursion and that cheered him.

70

He had picked up a nice illustrated edition of Marian McNeill's *A Scots Kitchen* and a smaller accompanying edition of *A Scots Cellar* for Lynn Landemar. For his great aunt Euphemia he had found *A Short History of Cupar and the Parish of Kettle*. And for himself he had purchased a nice copy of John Bulloch's history of the Pynours—the ancient guild of Aberdeen shore porters. Number fifty-four of one hundred numbered copies on hand-made paper. There was an old engraving in the book of porters unloading casks of whisky at the shore front in Leith, It reminded him of the drug smuggling case he had once investigated at the Leith docks with his friend Nigel Stonelaw:

Curiously enough, when Hamish left the shop who should he run into but the very same Inspector Nigel Stonelaw— of the Edinburgh and Lothians Police.

'Ah, Nigel,' he said, what are we up to today. Investigating a case in the pubic triangle?' The pubic triangle was the name the locals usually gave to a small knot of bars at the top of West Port offering strippers and lap dancers.

'Oh, good Lord, no,' said Stonelaw, 'Certainly not! Day off, in fact. Thought I'd go a walk, down through the Grassmarket and maybe through the Canongate to the Scottish Parliament.'

'You're not out shopping, then, or putting up the Christmas tree?'

Stonelaw shook his head and tutted a little. 'No. Well, to tell the truth, I'm sick of the shopping and the house has just gone mad, what with the daughter and son-in-law and the grandchildren all there. And there's been a bit of a hoo-ha this morning. Thought I'd escape for a while.'

'What sort of hoo-ha?' asked Hamish.

'Something quite ridiculous, actually. A sack of potatoes has disappeared! We bought them yesterday for today's dinner. The wife's made a big steak and kidney pie. But no potatoes. She says I should investigate it. As if I didn't have enough investigating to do!'

He looked at Hamish with a wry smile. 'Well, what do you think, Hamish. Is this a mystery that you can solve for us?'

'Perhaps not,' said Hamish, 'but why don't we ask the cleverest man in Edinburgh?'

'The cleverest man in Edinburgh?'

'Oh, yes,' said Hamish. The cleverest man in Edinburgh —Hamish Cawdor. He's written twenty books, one of them a history of the whole world! I saw him pass just a minute ago and I bet he's going to the Blue Blazer, just around the corner.'

The Blue Blazer was an old fashioned corner pub in the shadow of Edinburgh Castle. It was all mahogany, brass and stained glass. Inside there was a well-stocked gantry, traditional round tables and church pews for seats. At the corner of the bar sat a bearded man reading a slim book contemplatively and dripping fag ash on the bar. He was dressed in a worn Barbour jacket, a lumpy knitted jumper and his shirt collar was buttoned incorrectly so that one side was higher than the other.

'Good afternoon, Hamish,' said Hamish.

'Ah, Hamish, it's yourself,' said the second Hamish.

'This is my friend Nigel Stonelaw. He has an interesting query about potatoes.'

'Potatoes! The fruit of the sun. Literally, you know. The Incas, who discovered them, named them solanus, after the sun god, Sol. The Gaels used to call them buntats. In Shakespeare's England they were a delicacy, roasted in a clay oven.'

'My goodness,' said Stonelaw, 'you know a lot about potatoes, then.'

'Unfortunately not a great deal. But if you want to know more there is a great book—*The History and Social Influence of the Potato*, by Redcliffe Salaman. A mighty tome, more than seven hundred pages!'

'How could anyone write all that about potatoes?

'Ah, well, *there's* a story! It's told that Salaman—who was a Cambridge don—was diagnosed with a wasting disease and retired to the country. But the doctor was wrong! He lived long and prospered and decided to devote his time to the study of the humble potato. That's true academic dedication.' Hamish Cawdor frowned a little. 'He is not quite right, however, in his depiction of the Highlands of Scotland.'

'But potatoes have played a great part in the history of the British Isles, haven't they?' asked Hamish.

'Indeed,' replied Hamish Cawdor, 'some say that stock markets have crashed and people starved because of them— and in a way it's true. But we shouldn't blame the simple tattie for it. Politics and economics and just low down skulduggery play a part in all such things.'

'Anyway,' said Hamish, 'perhaps we can help solve Nigel's little mystery.' And he related the story of the strange disappearance of the Stonelaw family potatoes.

Well,' said Hamish Cawdor, 'maybe we need to know more about these disappearing potatoes.'

'For example,' said Hamish, 'what variety were they—Arran Comet, Pentland Squire, Ulster Banner, Catriona… '

'Ah yes,' said Hamish Cawdor, 'there are some fine spuds there, and in the old days you could get White City and Black

Yams… or even Lumpers or Irish Apples!'

'I haven't the faintest idea,' said Stonelaw, nonplussed. 'I thought they were just potatoes!'

'Alas, too many people do these days,' said Hamish Cawdor. The supermarkets package them as if they were all the same, and yet they are quite different!'

'Here,' said a little man in a bunnet who was standing at the bar next to them, I know a story about tatties… a good Scots story—about tatties and Rabbie Burns!'

'Do you, Jimmy,' said Hamish Cawdor, 'and whereabouts did you get that?'

'Och, I think it was when I was a mowdiewarp up in the Mearns, years ago. There was a lad who was a great one with the horses. They said he was a whisperer and he had the Word. He was a right clown, though. Always raring for a laugh.'

'Tell us it, then.'

'Oh, well. This is how he tellt it to me:

'One night after carousing a wee while, we got to talking about Rabbie Burns and how the museums aw had locks o' his hair and stuff like that.

"Wheest', he said, 'never mind aw they fal-di-rols, come wi' me and I'll show you some relics o' the bard'.

'Then he went under his bunk and he took out something that looked like an auld rotten parsnip. Then what do you think he said. He said, 'that's the shoulder bone o' Rabbie Burns!'

"Dinna be daft', I said.

"Honest as God's ma witness,' he said, 'and look here.' He took out what looked like some withered carrots. 'And that's the finger bones o' Rabbie Burns.'

'Then he took out an auld blackened turnip wi' holes in it.

74

'That's the skull o' Rabbie Burns', he said, 'dug up frae the mausoleum in Dumfries tae measure his heid!'

"Ach, you're taking a lend o' me,' I said 'Naw, naw,' he says. 'Wait. This is the last thing I hae tae show ye.'

'And he takes out two wee round white tatties. 'What do you think these are,' he says.'

Jimmy stopped telling the story to buttonhole the company. 'And what do you think I said?'

They all looked nonplussed.

'Well, I said 'Rabbie Burns's… ' And he said, 'Naw, King Edward's… "

Jimmy laughed at this so much that his bunnet fell off the back of his head, but he caught it dexterously behind his back as if it had happened many times before.

'Never mind your stories, ye daft auld gowk,' said a stout woman who was sitting at a stool by the bar. 'A tattie is a fine thing,' she continued. 'When we were travelling the road up in Buchan we'd eat nothing but tatties. We'd roast them over the camp fire and tell songs and sing stories. Those were the days. I mind them weel.'

'Do you know any songs about tatties?' asked Hamish.

'I certainly do,' she said. 'Here's one I learned on the berryfields of Blair. The tattie's the prince o' Scottish fare and the herring is the king of the sea! Mind you join in the chorus.'

And she launched into a song which went:

'Noo your hard working Scotsman's gone crazy, I fear,
Each day he maun have his bit beef and his beer,
But he disnae ken, though he may be nae caring,
His natural food it is tatties and herring.

Tatties and herring, tatties and herring.

Your natural food it is tatties and herring.
With a pound in the week, you maun aye be content,
Ten bob tae lay by for the claes and the rent,
Hauf a croon ye aye can be sparin',
You've seven an' sixpence for tatties an' herring.

When the Queen wanted someone tae fecht wi her foe,
It wisnae awa tae the lowlands she goes,
But awa' tae the hills for the brave an' the daring,
The lads that were fed upon tatties an' herring .

On Alma's Heights now the Russians they said,
We were forced tae tak heed o' the kilt and the plaid,
But they didnae ken 'twas the brave an' the daring,
The lads that were fed upon tatties an herring.

When the harbour o refuge was first spoken about,
Aiberdeen and Stonehaven they were fairly pit out,
For the Queen kent the convicts wid get their best faring,
Upon Buchan tatties an' Peterheid herring.'

Hamish smacked his thigh and said 'Och, that's a beauty, Jeannie.'

'Aye,' she said. 'Those were rare old times. Nowadays, what do you get? Fush and chips and deep fried Mars bars! She shook her head... and pot noodles and oven chips an microwave curries. All a load of rubbish and no good for you at all.'

'I couldn't agree with you more,' said Hamish Cawdor.

'Children today have never sat at a camp fire or sang a song. They just sit at home and watch DVDS and play with their

Gameboys and wi-fi. In my opinion… ' He gave Hamish and Stonelaw a huge wink, ' …the old-pastimes are still the best!'

They had a fine time in the Blue Blazer that afternoon and had a couple of drams and a few pints of Deuchars IPA for Stonelaw. They sang some more songs and told a couple of stories. 'Now, Hamish', said Hamish Cawdor, 'what sort of a whisky would you recommend to go with a tattie?'

'Well,' said Hamish, 'some potatoes have pretty flowers, but they are very poisonous and no animal will eat them except for the roe deer… and although Ayrshire new potatoes are delicious, boiled and served hot and with a little salt and butter, I can't think of a flavour that is anything like them.' He paused to consider. 'However,' he said, 'I do know that the finest potatoes in the world come from Caithness, up by the Flow Country. And I see up on the gantry a very fine old malt from a Caithness distillery—Pulteney. A fine peaty, full-bodied malt with a slight sensation of heather and honey! I think we may well have three of those.'

A little later, when Hamish and Stonelaw were heading away down Lothian Road. Hamish asked, 'Did you enjoy our little excursion this afternoon?'

'Oh, yes. It was very illuminating,' said Stonelaw. 'However, it's a pity that the cleverest man in Edinburgh couldn't solve our potato riddle.'

'Oh, no?' said Hamish, 'I thought he had.'

Stonelaw looked astonished. 'What do you mean?'

'Well, didn't he say that 'the old pastimes are still the best'!'

'Yes, but I don't see what that has to do with it!'

'Ah, well just walk a little further and I'll explain.'

By this time they were just coming to the window of a toy

shop called Wonderland. They stopped and Hamish pointed to something in the display.

'There we are—Mr Potato Head. An old children's toy. I played with it when I was a boy. You get the plastic pieces and you push them into a potato—eyes, nose, etc—to make a head, then you can add little arms and legs. It's made quite a revival recently. All the children want one. Including, I suppose, your grandchildren!'

Stonelaw looked puzzled and then his face lightened as he suddenly comprehended. He broke into a laugh, 'The little rascals!'

And, sure enough, when he returned home, there was the sack of potatoes in the wardrobe of the spare bedroom, and so were several little potato men.

THE FOOT OF THE WALK MURDERS

Chief Superintendent Robert Ord, who had grown rather corpulent in the years approaching his retirement, had puffed and panted his way up three flights of stairs to Hamish McDavitt's top floor flat in Royal Terrace, but on arrival he had been amply rewarded with both a hot cup of Assam tea and a dram of a nice fifteen-year-old Scapa that Hamish had purchased from a limited edition cask at the Malt Whisky Society.

As they sat in comfort by the balconied windows overlooking a cold and grey day to the north over the Firth, the conversation eventually got round to Ord's keenest interest—the history of criminology.

'Have you read the new book by Timothy Peers-David, *The True Story of the Edinburgh Ripper*?'

'Ah,' said Hamish, going across to his desk and retrieving a medium thickness volume in a fairly lurid dust jacket. 'Strange that you should mention it. In fact, it has just arrived—a gift from the author. I met him some time ago, when I was looking into the affair of the Halfway House haunting. I've glanced at it, but I haven't read it in any detail yet.' He put the book down on the barley twist gate-leg dining table in the centre of the room that, in truth, was seldom used for dining and was usually covered with books and papers. 'However,' Hamish continued, 'I believe that the author has discovered some new evidence and come up with a startling new theory.'

'Well, new theories seem to be de rigeur for these young authors. And there isn't much new evidence—at least not that I would credit a jot. We simply agreed to give him access to the old declassified police files. As usual, there isn't much attempt to give credit to good old-fashioned police work. In my view the original investigator of the case, Inspector John Lambie, solved the crime years ago, that's why, in a way, it has never been studied as much as some more sensational cases.'

This was true, as Hamish himself knew The 'Edinburgh Ripper' murders had pre-dated the infamous Whitechapel murders—also known as the Jack the Ripper murders—and had originally been known as the Foot of the Walk murders having taken place in or around the north end of Leith Walk, colloquially known as 'the foot of the walk'. The 'Ripper' appellation had only been added years later. Yet, despite the sensational nature of the crimes, their impact on the popular consciousness had been fairly limited, perhaps because the case had been solved and the perpetrator—a Lascar sailor known as Johnny Monkey—having committed suicide, had never gone to trial. It was probably also the case that the conservative Edinburgh press, with a reputation as more staid and serious than, say, the London newspapers with their gaudy illustrations and lurid supplements, had failed to publicise the murders properly, as well as completely ignoring their prurient sexual nature.

The book in question covered the best known facts of the case thoroughly and gave a very atmospheric description of the Edinburgh of 1886:

'Edinburgh in 1886: the Edinburgh of Stevenson's Jekyll and Hyde. The pest-ridden slums of the old town living hand in hand with the lavish terraces of the New Town. A busy birling city, gentlemen in their fine capes and canes, their servants, workmen of all appellations all jostling to do their business in the sometimes dusty, sometimes muddy streets. It was a city that had reached its apogee, and was now dwarfed by its rapacious neighbour to the west, force fed with Irish immigrants, hot steel, docks and railyards. But Edinburgh was still the Athens of the North and still Scotland's capital, and more than that, the capital of North Britain, its premier citizens aligning themselves with a unionist rather than a nationalist view of its place in the great British Empire… '

'It was the year of the Great Exhibition, wasn't it?' asked Hamish.

'The International Exhibition of Science, Art and Industry on the Meadows,' elaborated Ord. 'My parents always pointed out the entrance, the whalebone arch in Meadow Walk, when we went on walks after Sunday School. It's the only bit that still stands, although the whole thing must have been very impressive in its time.'

'There was a whole street, square and precinct built called 'Old Edinburgh' based on buildings that had been lost at that time. It's difficult for us to realise. We think that Edinburgh is old enough already, but some of the Old Town was being demolished then! It was preserved in the drawings of Bruce Home, but also in the reconstructed village Edinburgh built in the Meadows. There's a model in Huntly House, and we have the photographs of Marshall Wane to remind us.'

Hamish paused and thought for a moment.

'In fact, I have them here', he said. He stepped over to a bookcase and brought out an album of postcards from a drawer.

81

He presented Ord with a leather-bound album containing about twenty postcards, some in sepia, some colour tinted, some plain, and some with an inscription or a few words written on the front, as was the custom in those days.

'These are Marshall Wane's photographs of Old Edinburgh: The House of Mary o' Guise, Sympson's Close, the Old Tolbooth, the Scottish Mint, etcetera. Wane took them for the exhibition, but he kept the negatives. Fifteen years later the postcard was invented. So he recycled them all as postcards and made himself a few bob. It's a very strange set, I find. It's supposedly 'old' Edinburgh, yet all these buildings were built specially for the exhibition and demolished immediately afterwards. It's as artificial as a Disney stage set!'

Ord flicked through the album. All the scenes, set against the reconstructed buildings, featured burghers, or servants or fishwives posed around the set.

'Of course,' eventually added Ord, 'there is a link to the case. I believe it has been suggested that all of the victims were employed at the exhibition as models, and that Johnny Monkey may have worked on the construction of it. He may have met them there.'

'So, in fact,' added Hamish, 'the faces of some of the fishwives we see posing here could be those of the victims themselves!'

Ord hesitated. 'It's a queer thing, looking at old photos like these and for all we know we may be gazing into the eyes of someone who is shortly to be murdered. It's quite thought-provoking.'

'It's a queer thing altogether looking at any photo, perhaps,' said Hamish. 'All the people pictured in these photographs are long dead. But no-one remains as they are pictured. We all age and eventually die. Because a photograph is a frozen moment in time. A moment that can never be recovered— perhaps that is why photographs fascinate us.'

Ord looked a little disconcerted for a moment. Perhaps the thought of all and sundry as inevitable victims of the final Reaper was too much for him to contemplate, but then he rallied. 'We'll keep these for further discussion,' he said, 'but let's plod on with the Ripper case.'

The book gave a fair outline of the case itself. The fact of the matter was that in late August of 1886, three murders had been committed around the area of Leith at the bottom of Leith Walk. On the fifteenth of August, Annie Sloan, a poor but respectable scullery maid, had been discovered brutally murdered in a dark alley behind the Kirkgate. On the twenty-sixth of August, the body of Elsie Pierce, described as a 'drudge', but almost certainly a prostitute plying her trade around the area of the docks, had been found in a derelict back yard in Giles Street. The final victim, Mary McCutcheon, found on the thirty-first of August, had been similarly despatched, but there were some small differences in her case. She had come from a slightly better family than the others and had a decent job as a housekeeper in the Mount Royal Hotel in Princes Street. She had been found in a washhouse behind a townhouse in Pilrig Street, nearer Edinburgh and the New Town. She had also been pregnant at the time of her death.

The cases had caused a great panic on the streets of Edinburgh and Leith, but the press reports had rather glossed over the full horror of the crimes: 'All the ladies that have met their unfortunate end have been shamefully violated in a way that no lady of either high or humble birth should be. They had faced their Maker in the commission of the unspeakable act and had been finally dispatched with the aid of a common gutting knife ubiquitously carried in the Port of Leith by fishermen, dockers and sailors.'

In fact, as Peer-David's book made clear, with the aid of some shockingly graphic photographs rescued from the police archive, the poor victims had been brutally sodomised whilst held around the throat. Before the end of the ordeal, the murderer had used his other hand, and his knife, to violently rip open their stomach, practically disembowelling them. The pathologist's reports were detailed in the book and were of particular interest. In fact the first two examinations had been conducted by probably the most famous medical practitioner in Edinburgh at that time, Joseph Bell, a lecturer at Edinburgh University. Bell was an innovative surgeon who developed a system of deduction in examining medical cases.

He was said to have been the inspiration for Arthur Conan Doyle's fictional detective, Sherlock Holmes. The third examination, due to Bell's absence on university business, had been undertaken by his almost equally well known colleague, Dr Vincent Imrie, a giant of a man who delighted in the grisliness of his occupation and had been known both for the vigour with which he pursued his profession and his non-conformity to the social mores of the time. To, illustrate this, Peers-David had included a caricature portrait of him from the *London Illustrated News* showing him brandishing an extremely vicious-looking dissecting knife above a partially dissected corpse as his students fainted in circle around him.

They spent a moment or two glancing at the illustrations, 'Classic sex crimes,' commented Ord. 'Obviously the perpetrator could only achieve a climax through an extremely violent act. We know a great deal more about such murders these days, but in those days such things weren't really spoken of; it seemed all too impossibly horrific for the Victorian middle-classes to stomach. And there were few advanced tests available, no DNA tests or anything of that nature. There was no psychological profiling, nothing like that.'

In fact, none of these techniques had proved necessary. The common and accepted solution to the case was succinctly outlined in the book. The case had been solved, apparently, by one of the most renowned Scottish detectives of the day, Chief Inspector John Lambie, on the very same day as the last murder.

'Lambie, a great figure', said Ord, 'A real policeman's policeman.'

Lambie had solved the case by sheer hard detective work, pounding the streets and interviewing prostitutes, dockers, mollycoddlers; anyone who might have observed the least thing. Lambie had a formidable reputation as an Edinburgh detective, tireless, dedicated, unafraid to enter even the most debauched den of the dark side of the city. He was reputedly equally respected and feared by both his own colleagues and the criminal underworld of Edinburgh. It was said that he had personally arrested half the criminals brought to justice in the 80s and had rid the city forever of the scourge of baby-farming. It was also reported that, not content to sit at his desk and await the results of his investigations, he disguised himself as a tramp or a beggar and trod the streets himself seeking informants. For this and other reasons, he was also sometimes mooted as a model for Conan Doyle's Sherlock Holmes.

Through his endeavours, Lambie had traced the source of the affair to a Lascar sailor named Johnny Syed but commonly known as Johnny Monkey, who, it had been revealed, had been seen near the scene of the first two crimes. On the day of the final murder, Lambie had also discovered that the suspect was wanted for similar crimes in another seaport. He had sent a squad to the suspect's lodgings to arrest him, but Johnny Monkey had felt the hot breath of the hounds of justice and had hanged himself before they arrived. The evidence of Johnny Monkey's guilt, even though purely circumstantial, was universally accepted and no further such murders took place in Leith for some time-not, in fact, until the Tower Bar Taproom affair of 1908.

'The rest of the book,' said Hamish, 'puts together a rather unconvincing case for another perpetrator, but as usual, relies on the old ploy of an establishment cover-up to protect a respectable gentleman.'

'As if the police had enough time—as well as the sheer lack of integrity—to spend half their time covering up for the failings of the upper classes,' sighed Ord, who both favoured and loyally supported his own policemen while discreetly maintaining a veiled contempt for the Edinburgh establishment and their machinations.

The True Story of the Edinburgh Ripper claimed that the murders were actually committed by a supposedly respectable Edinburgh physician, Iain Ewing Valentine, who was vaguely related to the Duke of Buccleuch.

There were three main arguments to the case against Valentine: Firstly, his profession had resulted in him spending a great deal of time in the vicinity of the murders. Secondly, he would have carried a knife that would have been suitable for the commission of the crimes. Thirdly, and crucially according to the book, he had been carrying out a specialist branch of his profession (that involved meeting a great many women) that had been relatively common at the time but little known about today. In fact, to illustrate this, Peers-David included the page of a pamphlet that advertised 'the latest and most pertinent treatment for hysteria, pelvic hyperemia and congestion of the genitalia; carried out with the revolutionary patented vibrating machine and applied under full medical supervision.'

'What exactly was wrong with these women?' asked Ord

Hamish allowed himself a little chuckle. 'Largely nothing at all, or what we nowadays call sexual frustration. It was not uncommon practice for doctors to attend to women—mostly married women—in this way. Invariably they would do it conscientiously and exercise discretion despite what the more sensationalist accounts may say.'

'So could this have any connection with the sexual perversions of the murderer?'

Hamish's brow creased for a moment, but then there was a little shake of his head. 'Whatever we may think about the legitimacy of these methods, it's hard to see what the connection is. Can we really acquaint giving women pleasure with brutally murdering them! And, besides, the women victims of these crimes could hardly afford that sort of exclusive treatment.'

'Has it any relevance, then?'

Hamish smiled: 'Only, I would suggest, of making the book a little more interesting for the reader!'

Which… ' Ord added, is only too commonplace these days!'

Secondly, the author had examined all of Valentine's recorded correspondence which he had discovered in the

National Library and he had seemingly unearthed evidence for his crimes—coded in anagram form within the letters!

For example, one letter seemed to deal with his purchase of crab meat from the harbour at Newhaven and Peers-David had selected a couple of sentences: 'I have the taste for partan meat... Do send aunt a live one... '

This had been sorted to read: 'I have a taste for meat... Anne Sloan d(eceased) due to I. E. V. [Iain Ewing Valentine]'

'Sheer nonsense,' ejaculated Ord, and Hamish nodded in fervent agreement. 'I've seen this sort of trickery a couple of times before, but it's just a game and means nothing. It must have taken Peers-David some time to work out these convoluted puzzles, but anyone could do it if they worked hard enough.'

The third part of the argument, however, was a little more interesting. There were a couple of mentions in the police investigation into the case of the last victim, Mary McCutcheon, of a hitherto unconsidered piece of evidence.

Apparently, in the last days before her sudden death, she had been noticed wearing a ring with the initials IV. Finally, on top of this, there was a suggestion that McCutcheon had been examined by a physician appointed by her family in the early days of her pregnancy and, although there was no direct evidence, Peers-David harnessed some reasonably convincing secondary sources to suggest it may have been Valentine himself.

'There is a point here', said Ord, 'The testimony of the witnesses is recorded, although no ring was found with the body. If the book has a virtue, it is in bringing this loose end of the evidence to the fore.'

'OK, I suppose', said Hamish, 'But I'm also interested in

the published photos and I haven't seen these before.'

'Well, you're the photography expert.'

'Perhaps in the social history of photography, But as regards the history of crime photography. You know a wee bit about that, don't you?'

'Well, yes, suppose. Photography was reluctantly accepted during the mid-nineteenth century by the diehards. However, there's no doubt that its uses in archiving images of criminals, recording crime scenes, and as a forensic tool were instrumental in the development of modern criminology and worked hand-in-hand with other innovatory techniques such as Henry Faulds's development of fingerprinting.'

'There were other techniques developed—eugenics, for example?'

'Pash,' said Ord, 'A load of silly nonsense. Galton, who was a moderate criminologist, had the daft idea that you could use composite photos to identify a typical criminal likeness. If you could, any policeman would tell you, it would make their job a hell of a lot easier. They could just arrest all the ugly mugs and bow and curtsey to the angelic faces! Then there was the even sillier idea that murderers and their victims had some sort of facial resemblance that could be detected. And then there was the endless photographing of hands and feet, fingers and toes, in the belief that you could identify criminal characteristics in those alone... Here, look at some of the examples in Peers-David's book... ' He opened the book at a centre spread of glossy black and white photographs.

'Now', said Ord, 'here are some useful if rather graphic forensic photographs, showing a comparative view of the bodies of the three victims laid out flat. Look, you can see the remarkable similarity of the jagged diagonal cut in their abdomen that Peers-David claims attests to the left-handedness of the murderer. The photographic record means that a detective has evidence of the nature of the offence without personally having to accompany the pathologist on the investigation of each body. On the other hand,' he said, turning the page, 'here are the photographs of the deceased Johnny Monkey, showing his face from three angles with inked on dimensions, and of his hands, palm uppermost.'

'Why is there a deep bruise on his forehead?' asked Hamish, suddenly perking up and furrowing his brow in the rather exaggerated way that indicated he was concentrating.

'Oh, apparently, the rope that he had hanged himself with had broken or become undone and he had fallen against the hearth. That was how he was found, lying face down with his head bashed and his neck crushed by the heavy rope.'

Hamish scanned the images again for a moment intently, screwing his eyes together and scratching his chin. Then he rose suddenly and went to his desk, fetching a magnifying glass. He laid the book flat on an occasional table with a desk lamp to avoid direct light from the windows and, meticulously, scanned both of the hands of Johnny Monkey with the glass, then, equally carefully, each elevation of the face. Ord knew better than to interrupt him until he looked up, thoughtfully, a minute or two later.

'Have you seen something, Hamish?'

Hamish's thoughtfulness vanished and he suddenly seemed quite lively.

'Yes, indeed. This man, from the evidence of these photographs, cannot have been the murderer of those poor women!'

Ord was suitably impressed by the forcefulness of this

declaration and his eyes opened wide: 'Good God, man. You're not suggesting that you can tell that from the hands and the face? Was all that Victorian mumbo-jumbo right, do you think! That the imprint of the murderer is contained within his features?'

Hamish laughed. 'No, no, nothing as fanciful, I'm afraid. Something much simpler than that. A working seaman will be commonly using knives, irons and other nautical tools. We can see if we look closely that his right hand is slightly thicker and more calloused than the left. Also, if we look closely at the face, the right-hand side has slightly more of a shadow than the left. This is common when shaving with a cutthroat razor—drawing the blade across the face from the opposite side is more efficient and shaves closer. I conclude, therefore, that this man is right-handed. And yet, Timothy Peers-David has concluded from the evidence that the culprit was definitely left-handed!'

Ord thought for a minute about this and slowly nodded his appreciation. 'So, do you think that it is, in fact, possible that Valentine was the murderer?'

Hamish shook his head. 'No, there's nothing yet strong enough to allow us to assume that, and I have noticed that although Peers-David makes a point about the left-handedness of the murderer, I haven't yet come across his evidence that Valentine was left-handed.' He shrugged. 'Although, of course, it might be found on a closer reading of the book, I just don't know.'

Hamish walked to the window and looked out towards a sky turning dark and stormy. He added, 'But I do think that the case merits our further attention! Do you think we could have a closer look at the police file?'

'I'll trump that. I'll have the whole thing taken round to my place. Tomorrow's Sunday, and we can spend a fine day together with a special old malt I've been saving for you and try our hand at cracking an old mystery.'

So at lunchtime the next day, Hamish strolled down to Ord's townhouse in Royal Terrace. Royal Terrace, being the most southerly of a succession of grand New Town terraces, was more secluded and a little gloomier than the rest, facing north into a belt of trees and a modernist new build that belonged to one of the many Edinburgh insurance houses. The buildings were impressive, but not quite as 'groomed' as those in Great King or Northumberland Street. Some of the railings were a little rusted and the sandstone flaking in places. The elm and lime trees shaded the terrace from the already diffuse northern light. In the gutters were the decaying remnants of some fallen leaves. Ord's house was fairly central and had flagstone steps well-worn from centuries of use. The large solid door was a rather shabby black and there was an old bell pull rather than the modern buzzer systems. Ord had lived here for many years, the greater part of his adult life. And he had needed a large house, bringing up six children along with his wife who had, sadly, died of a sudden pulmonary embolism some four years previously. All of the children were away from home now, but Ord kept the place much as it was, awaiting the increasingly less frequent visits of the children as they extended their acquaintance with more far-flung parts of the world. One concession Ord had made recently was to rent out the basement portion of the house to two students at Edinburgh University. He occasionally complained about the noise they made but Hamish sensed that he appreciated the liveliness they brought to the old place.

As usual, Ord ushered Hamish into the drawing room of the house which was huge. There was a large black marble fireplace and a matching ebonised boudoir grand piano. The walls were covered in framed memorabilia of Ord's career and the sofas were topped with ornate Victorian antimacassars. As usual, Ord offered Hamish a drink—today a special twenty year-old Macallan—but then, as always, he invited Hamish to join him in the kitchen, which was noticeably less tidy than the drawing room but much more lived in. Ord sank into a well-worn old armchair by the range and started to puff on his equally well-worn pipe.

'Sorry, Hamish, not a popular habit these days, but one of my great comforts.' He tapped the pipe against the shutters of the bay window. Well, time to settle into our dram and then. . .' He indicated with a sweep of his arm the kitchen table which was piled with the accumulated material on the Ripper cases.

There was a great deal that was of interest. Not just police record material but personal items also. There was a rather gory reminder; a mahogany box containing a length of the sisal rope that Johnny Monkey had used to hang himself, stained dark—supposedly with his blood. There was a framed photograph of John Lambie in the Masonic regalia of his Lodge: No 1 Lodge, St Mary's Chapel, Hill Street. And also a peculiar item, a white glove, stamped with a police insignia and framed. An inscription read 'Presented by Edinburgh City Police to Inspector Lambie on the occasion of the passing of one week in his precinct without an arrest, 10th March 1885.'

'That's a rare item. It was an unusual custom of the time,' remarked Ord. 'I think this was the only one ever presented.

But there was probably good reason for it. It was the winter of the great freeze and the criminals were too bollocks-cold to go thieving, never mind the police to catch them!'

'Did Lambie not keep his own memorabilia?' asked Hamish. 'With such a distinguished career, surely he would have wanted to retain some reminders.'

'Apparently not, but remember he left the Force at the beginning of 1887, quite prematurely. Then he did rather well for himself. Married the heiress of the Waterson family of pen nib manufacturers. Never had to work again. Probably forgot all about his earlier career.'

More importantly, there was Lambie's casebook on the Ripper murders—a long narrow ledger, each page meticulously filled with precise details of the investigation in a distinctive spidery left to right sloping handwriting.

Each item was numbered and there was a system of cross referencing—forwards in the right margin and backwards in the left margin—that Hamish found quite ingenious. There was no doubt that he was a dedicated, if not obsessive man.

There were the three pathologists' reports, typewritten by what was probably an early Remington treadle typewriter, but annotated with the sprawling script that is often associated with the medical profession and initialled by both Bell and Imrie. Ord read them carefully while Hamish was similarly examining Lambie's casebook. He was hoping that they might comment directly on the imputed left or right-handedness of the murderer, but none of them did. It could only be presumed that this had been concluded from a more recent examination of the forensic photographs.

Finally, there was a square wooden box which contained the glass plates of the photographs they had seen illustrated in the Peers-David book. Hamish latched on to these with particular interest, taking each out in turn, holding it up to the light of a watery winter sun that had begun to angle through the south-facing kitchen window, then laying it flat on top of a piece of white paper and examining it with his glass.

After a while, he seemed a little more agitated, and returned to three plates several times in return. Eventually, he sat back in his chair and raised his eyes to the ceiling with a shake of the head and a shrug or, almost, a little laugh.

'Bob, Bob, I have been totally misled, I'm afraid. Not my own fault really, more a failure of the publishers to appreciate the technology of the times. Look at these.'

He took out two of the glass plates, they were inscribed on the frame 'J Begbie & Sons, Leith St.'

'Sometimes, quite outdated modes of photograph were used until the equipment or the materials ran out. Also, photographers didn't quite distinguish in the early days between their illustrious clients and the mere criminal. That's why some mugshots are in ornate frames in the early days.

'These are the forensic photographs of Annie Sloan and Elsie Pierce. They are taken using the ambrotype method. Now, the ambrotype worked by using a glass plate negative and then pressing or pasting a piece of black velvet behind it to reverse the tones, making it appear like a positive image. The velvet has been scraped off these, but you can feel where it has been. Here.'

Ord took and examined the photographs, blowing a little dust from them as he did so.

'The publishers who have reproduced these plates have not fully understood the technology involved, however. They have taken them to be genuine negatives and reproduced them on this basis!'

'I think I see what you're getting at!' said Ord.

'Yes, the photographs in the book are actually a mirror image of what was intended. So the contention that a left-handed murderer murdered these two girls is incorrect!'

'So we've been led down a blind alley.' Ord seemed quite disheartened. Then perhaps it was Johnny Monkey after all! Good work… but a bit disappointing.… I suppose.'

Hamish hesitated, and when he spoke it was in a rather deliberate fashion.

'Yes, I have no doubt that Johnny Monkey was the murderer of these girls. There is some evidence and he was proven to be of a violent disposition—but the enigma certainly doesn't end there!'

'What do you mean?'

'The third photograph, of Mary McCutcheon, is by another photographer. It's inscribed 'Jas Auld & Ptnr, Princes St.' And it's the equivalent of a calotype, which means a positive print is taken each time from a glass negative. Now, unless the photographers have got it wrong, and I suspect it is unlikely that they would have, being much more scrupulous in their day than we are in ours, this photograph is reproduced correctly in the Peers-David book.

Ord thought for a moment. 'Then that can only mean that the wound is of the opposite inclination to the first two!'

'Exactly, and that the third victim was butchered in an identical way, but by a left-handed man!'

They sat in silence for a few moments, unsure what make of this revelation.

'What do we do now, Hamish?'

'Well, I think we set ourselves for a long afternoon and

continue to go through this material more thoroughly.'

And so they did, with the aid of a continually brewing pot of tea and another dram and, eventually, with a rather pleasant meal of Chicken Cacciatore and a bottle of Barolo that Ord had send round from Umberto's—a practice in which, suspected Hamish, he commonly indulged at the weekend.

They sat back in their armchairs, full, content, but a little brain-weary from their exertions and their stomachs bloated from the richness of the food and drink.

Ord spoke first. 'I've been through just about everything, but I'm blowed if I can sort it out. It seems we may have a copycat killer, but why? And why that particular victim?' He let out his breath in a gesture of exasperation. 'Do you have any idea, Hamish?'

Hamish hesitated. 'I have an idea, but not yet fully formed. I was looking at Lambie's casebook. Do you notice that not all the entries leading up to the final entry are dated. But the final entry certainly is. Both a date and a time—6.30pm, 31st August 1886—and then a detailed account of the discovery of Johnny Monkey's body. And folded into the page, the crucial telegram from the Dublin Police, that had resulted from Lambie's enquiries and that associates him with sexual crimes—but with something missing' He passed the ledger book over to Ord.

'You're right, it seems that the top part of the telegram has been cut off, but it's just to make it fit the book, is it not?'

'Maybe, but you will note that the date on which the telegram was sent is missing. The only date we have is a hand-written date, the date on which it was purportedly received.'

'Does that mean something?'

Hamish shook his head slightly. He looked a little weary.

'I think it may, but I can't quite piece it all together tonight. There are still some contradictions that I can't quite resolve.' He creased his brows in an exaggerated way that looked almost painful. 'I feel that we're almost halfway to a solution, but I just can't fully picture it yet.'

'But,' interjected Ord, 'we have made some progress. For a start, we now suspect that the third murder was committed in a different way to the first two… '

'Yes', admitted Hamish, 'there could be several reasons for that—it could be a copycat murder, there could be accomplices involved, or even a clever way of deliberately disguising the modus operandi.'

He rose, a little stiffly, to his feet. 'There are a few things that remain uncertain. The missing information about the exact circumstances of the run-up to the discovery of Johnny's supposed suicide… and the whole matter of the mysterious disappearing ring, presumably taken from the body of the final victim by the murderer.' He reached for his coat. 'I fear that we need to do a little more research which will have to wait until tomorrow.'

'What's that?'

'Well, I want to go to the National Library—to have a look at the letters of Dr Valentine—and I have a special task for you Bob, if you can lay aside your duties for another half day.'

'We're too far in the thick of it to stop now. What can I do?'

'I would like you to contact your Masonic friends and ask them this: in 1886, who would have done the catering for the Hill Street Lodge? It's a tricky one, but if anyone can find out, you can.'

Ord looked stupefied but nodded his agreement. He knew from experience that Hamish sometimes had a roundabout way of getting at the facts and that little side alleys sometimes led to his solutions. There was little point in questioning his intentions at this stage.

As Hamish walked along Royal Terrace to the bottom of Scotland Street, the lights seemed to dim, the little wind that always inhabited the streets of the New Town grew out of the calm and suddenly swirled around blowing a cold gust in his face. It was quiet, although some indistinct noises of drunken carousing could be discerned in the north towards Leith. For some reason, Hamish felt uncomfortable and quickened his step uphill towards Drummond Place. This was the heart of the New Town, where wall plaques noted the residences of famous inhabitants: Sydney Goodsir Smith, the poet, William McTaggart, the artist. Here the past and the present met.

And that was a feeling that plagued Hamish from time to time, the past suddenly impinging on the present. He knew that he had a talent for solving mysteries. Mostly, it was due to nothing that was particularly special—research, simple logic, a little knowledge of locality and history—but sometimes it required a kind of vision, an empathy, a sudden understanding of a lost or an unseen happening.

Hamish, with his mild-mannered demeanour, had always given the impression of being a secure and stable person, but to some extent that was an illusion, perhaps as it is for everyone,

Robert Ord was different. He was a good man, but also tough and determined. He had a very traditional, perhaps dated, sense of duty. He had spent a career mixing with the criminal underworld and it had hardened him. But Hamish was not so hard. He felt the cold wind stir again and intrude through the buttons of his overcoat. Suddenly in the empty street he felt a little afraid, as if someone was following him in the emerging dank November fog, He hurried along London Road and up into Broughton Street where a car or two could be heard in the distance but the shops and pubs were locked for the night.

At the heart of his unease was the feeling that he almost had a solution to the mystery of the Foot of the Walk murders—but it wasn't clear cut. It was not a simple problem like many he had solved before. But, strangely, although it was buried in the past, it felt immediate to him—as if the old bones of Edinburgh had dragged themselves from their burial grounds to walk the streets again.

He turned the corner into Royal Terrace and gratefully ascended the steps to his top floor flat. After securing the door, Hamish filled a glass with cold tap water and added n little liver salts to help clear his head. Before he retired he had another rake through *The True Story of the Edinburgh Ripper*. The last thing he focused on were photographs of some of the protagonists: Iain Valentine, a handsome fellow with slightly tousled hair and a look of schoolboy innocence; John Lambie, tall and serious-looking with thinning hair and a hooked nose; Joseph Bell, an avuncular figure with a whole head of white hair; Vincent Imrie, with a scowling expression on his enormous head and shoulders, framed by lamb-chop sideburns and dark hairs growing from his nostrils and below eyes; and Johnny Monkey, his face blank, drained and inhuman in death.

Hamish thought that he would sleep only fitfully, but he slept throughout the night, visited by strange and frightening dreams and, when he eventually awoke and saw a little glimmer of morning sun rise in the sky beyond Arthur's Seat, he looked up at the highest point of the south-facing case window and there he imagined he saw the face of the murderer of an innocent young woman.

The next day was sunny, if cold. The very last leaves of the autumn, now transformed to full-blown winter, were falling from the trees and swirling around the entrance to Ord's house as Hamish tugged at the old bell pull at around

Ord was glad to see him. 'You look quite sprightly, Hamish, a good morning's work?'

'OK, Bob, how about yourself?'

'Well. I've got what you want. It took a while, but Jim Carruthers found it. He's the one that keeps the website for the Lodge. Not really something I approve of myself, you know… ' There was an unspoken assumption between them that Ord, a long-time member of the Order himself, was a traditionalist who did not care to make Masonic matters explicit.

'And… '

'Oh, yes. The catering for the Lodge was almost certainly taken care of by the Mount Royal Hotel—only a few streets away.'

'Good. That doesn't surprise me.' Hamish seemed pleased. 'Now, let me show you what I have found.' Hamish produced a photocopy of a letter by Valentine from his jacket pocket and handed it to Ord.

'Don't bother reading it in detail. The contents aren't particularly important. It is a serious thing to accuse a man of murder, even a hundred years after his death, and I wanted to at least have a look at some of the material Peers-David had employed to make his case against Valentine.'

'And you found this letter?'

'I read through quite a lot of material. This particular letter doesn't have any peculiar anagrams or anything that I can see, but it tells us two simple things.'

'What precisely?'

'Firstly, there is a reference to 'Canongate Kilwinning'. We now know that Valentine, in common with many in his profession, was a Mason. That is his lodge. Secondly, look at the handwriting, neat and upright. In fact, rather more orderly than one would expect from a physician. But, I think you will accept that it is more than likely the handwriting of a right-handed, not a left-handed man. Look.... ' Hamish took from his pocket an old pen with a waverley nib and, meticulously mirrored the script, writing with his right hand to demonstrate that the loops and curls naturally followed the inclination of his fist.

Ord was convinced by the demonstration. 'Well, I presume we can confidently state that Valentine is no longer a suspect, then—at least for the first two murders?'

Hamish sat up straight in his armchair and placed his hands rather deliberately on his knees as if ready to make a pronouncement.

'Here is the logical path I have followed. Firstly, we can now accept, I think, that Johnny Monkey committed the first two murders. There is considerable circumstantial evidence and he is a man with a proven history of violence. Also, he had the time and the opportunity for both the first two murders and the recorded testimony seems to suggest so.'

'Also, of course, Hamish, doesn't the very fact that he took his own life on the same day as the last of his murders surely suggest his guilt in itself?'

'Yes, that would be the case, but it is not accidental that I have not included that suggestion in my logical deduction so far. In fact, examine that statement... he took his own life on the same day as the last of his murders There are two assumptions within that statement that I am not willing to accept!'

'I don't get you, Hamish. Wasn't that a key component of the case against him?'

'Bear with me a little longer, Bob. I'll try to show you how my reasoning has progressed, but I want to put my argument together in a coherent way.'

'Go on, then.'

'Well, if we now proceed from an acceptance that Johnny Monkey committed the first two murders, that takes us up to the twenty-sixth of August. Let's further examine what happened subsequently. My contention is that someone else was responsible for the other two murders and that that person would have to be completely familiar with the modus operandi of the first two. We just have to determine who this person is.'

Ord sat up suddenly. 'The other two murders! But surely there was just one more—that of Mary McCutcheon?'

'No. One of the first things that I found suspicious about the case was the inferred suicide of Johnny Monkey. He was a sailor by profession. Sailors have to be familiar with a range of knots. I couldn't accept that he botched the knot whereby hung the noose by which he hanged himself. Therefore, I concluded one of two things. Either he did not seriously intend to hang himself or, alternatively, he was actually murdered. The bruising on his head seemed to suggest the latter. It would have been easy for someone, someone he didn't suspect, perhaps disguised as a down-and-out or a fellow sailor, to knock him unconscious and then to hang him by the neck until he was throttled, finally releasing the noose to suggest a fall.'

'So the suspect murdered Mary McCutcheon then immediately came to the Lascar's lodgings and murdered him.'

'No, I don't think that is what happened. For the murderer —if my explanation is correct—that would have been too risky. Perhaps Johnny's body wouldn't have been found, perhaps he would have gone out on another murderous excursion of his own. My contention is that Johnny Monkey was murdered earlier in the day, then the murderer arranged to meet and subsequently slaughter Mary McCutcheon with the intention of laying the blame on his first victim. In order to do so, he must have known her well.'

'Well then,' said Ord, 'let me play the devil's advocate. Surely it can only have been Valentine. He knew her well, as we know—she wore his ring—and he frequented the same areas of Leith. Perhaps he found out something and then used the fake suicide of Johnny Monkey as an alibi for himself.'

'That seems to be possible, but I have to say I find the circumstantial evidence against Valentine flimsy to say the least. The mainstay of the case is the undisputed fact that she wore a ring with the initials IV' and the suggestion that that ring was given to her by the man who had made her pregnant—the man who, I contest, slaughtered her most bloodily because of that and also murdered Johnny Monkey to cover his crime!'

'If not Valentine, who then?'

'The business of the ring vexed me, as it was attested to in the transcript of the evidence. If it was indeed initialled, it would be a damning indictment of the murderer. Yet, would any gentleman in those days be so careless as to give a girl of lower station an initialled ring—such a key pointer to his identity—if he didn't want to be exposed? Then I thought, perhaps the ring was something similar, a more general token of her relationship. Now, remember that Mary was a waitress at the Mount Royal Hotel, as we now know only minutes from St Mary's Chapel and where gentlemen from the Lodge probably dined after their meetings. Suppose the ring was seen by her friends who were naïve about such matters. A Masonic ring with a set of compasses could easily have been mistaken for the letters 'IV'!

Ord started. 'Ah, so the culprit was a Mason?'

'Yes. Let us now construct an identity for the murderer. He was left-handed. He was a Mason. He had gotten this poor girl with child and now wanted rid of her—probably because he had another, more important, affair to consummate.

'He knew that Johnny Monkey had committed the first two murders and was in a position to murder him too to cover his tracks. He may have had some aptitude for disguise. He was a man of great insight, of nerve and ability. He was also a monster, an evil man who could, without compunction, rape and slaughter a young woman he had professed to love simply to further his own future. He was as wicked as the criminals he himself hunted and captured and took to trial!'

'John Lambie!' Ord gasped in astonishment.

'His own notes gave me the final clue. His spidery handwriting sloping to the left clearly indicated he was left-handed. He was, as we know from his memorabilia, a member

105

of the Hill Street Lodge who either dined at, or were served by the staff from, the Mount Royal Hotel—as you discovered yourself—where he presumably met Mary McCutcheon. Then there were the careful notes of the evidence he had collected. I asked myself, why were most of them not dated! And the crucial telegram from Dublin, which seemed the most definitive evidence, had had the date cut off. If that had been received a day or two earlier, then why hadn't Johnny Monkey been apprehended earlier? Now we know. The key piece of evidence, the clue that Lambie claimed had confirmed his guilt in his mind and led him to call the constables on the evening of the thirty-first of August was the only one that was both timed and dated in the notes. He needed time to set up his plan and ensure that he had committed both murders before the constable he had instructed found the body of Johnny Monkey. that evening

'Lambie had committed two brutal murders, but I believe that before doing so, he had the enterprise to pound the streets of Leith for a while until he found some lag or drunken sot who would claim, rightly or wrongly, to have seen Johnny Monkey at such and such a location. Then he simply sent a constable to interview him, thus concocting the evidence that enabled the supposed suicide to be discovered that night. The very night that it would be of use to Lambie, to cover his own foul crime! Finally, then, there is the circumstantial evidence.

'Throughout our investigation I was struck by the differences between the first two murders and the last and the evidence surrounding them. A different photographer and pathologist. Only Lambie could have arranged such things. He was smart and he didn't think it wise to have the same people at the scene of the third crime in case they noticed, not the similarity, but the difference from the other two!'

Ord seemed nonplussed. 'It is an astonishing revelation. Lambie was regarded as a pillar of the community. He dedicated his life to fighting crime. How could he do such a thing?'

'I don't think that either you or I can comprehend it. I can only think he must have been a very wicked man indeed.'

'Yes, to murder coldly and cruelly just for the pure purpose of self gain.'

'That is one way to look at it, yet it hardly suffices. To kill as violently and savagely as that someone who is bearing your own child, someone you have claimed to love. There is something that isn't just pragmatic, it is something that is bestial... pure evil.'

'And, of course, he got away with it.'

'Yes, it seems so.' Hamish collected himself for a moment. 'But what actually happened to Lambie—doesn't the book tell us?'

'It's related in the book. As I already mentioned, he left the Force and did get married to his sweetheart and inherited the family business. He moved to England where he helped with the company a while, but then he developed a canker of the brain. He deteriorated quite rapidly and died a couple of years later, in November 1888.'

Hamish reflected for a minute. 'Tell me, then, whereabouts in England did he move to?'

Ord flicked through the book, checking the index and then finding the correct page. 'Here it is: Islington.'

'Islington in north London?' Hamish shrugged. 'Not very far from Whitechapel, in fact.'

Silence and the weight of old whisky weighed heavily in

Ord's drawing room as he puffed away at his old pipe and they both contemplated, for while, books that could, or could not, be written.

A MYSTERIOUS AFFAIR AT
GAYFIELD HOUSE

Chief Inspector Robert Ord was in the meetings room at the New Town Trust Conference Centre at Gayfield House, just a few minutes walk from Princes Street and the bustle of the city rush hour. Gayfield House was a fine early eighteenth-century mansion that had once stood in its own substantial grounds but was now hemmed in by a variety of central city buildings. There were the Georgian terraces of Gayfield Square to the south, the Victorian tenements of East London Street, two bulky red sandstone schools and some nondescript garages and warehouses. Taxi drivers congregated by the garages and there was the smell of greasy burgers and oil slicks. A few hundred yards away, occasional cars turned into the modernist concrete block of the police station in Gayfield Square for various unknown purposes.

The meetings room itself was elegant and simply furnished with freshly painted magnolia walls and a grey knotted pile carpet. The north-facing wall featured three large sash windows framing the slate blue Edinburgh sky of a chilly winter's evening At one end of the room was an imposing streaked cream marble fireplace and at the other a more recent addition, a carved mahogany hearth in a secessionist style. In the centre was a large oak table with twelve carver chairs; against the window, three smaller tables covered with linen table clothes were set aside for catering. The most impressive feature of the room, however, was the six large framed sectional panoramas of Edinburgh arranged around the non-windowed walls of the room. These constituted the only complete original hand-coloured set of Robert Barker's famous panorama of 1775. Robert Barker, an Irishman resident in Edinburgh in the eighteenth century, had famously invented the panorama one day on nearby Calton Hill when he conceived the idea of a large painting covering the view around 360 degrees. His panoramas of Edinburgh and London were subsequently exhibited in purpose-built buildings in London and in Edinburgh on the Mound and became a popular entertainment of the late eighteenth and early nineteenth centuries.

Ord was there that evening in his capacity as chair of the projects sub-committee of the Playfair Association, an organisation committed to the preservation and renovation of old Edinburgh

The rest of the sub-committee were also gathered. The secretary was Liz McLaughlin, a blousy woman in her early fifties with infeasibly large spectacles, a jowly face and bright red lips. McLaughlin was a councillor for one of the southside Edinburgh wards. She was the sort of person who either knew or wanted to know everything that was going on in the city. Bureaucracy and gossip equally occupied her time which seemed to be unlimited. Due to her untiring enthusiasm she was often in the news, and never far behind when controversy beckoned. So far, however, she had managed to avoid association with any of the numerous scandals that afflicted local politics in Edinburgh. Both her friends and her enemies found her tiresome but hard to ignore.

The Monypennys were there. Gordon Monypenny was the younger son of an entrepreneurial family who had, between them, had an interest in a variety of Edinburgh commercial affairs. Gordon's latest involvement was in a company called City Days who arranged expensive corporate outings and exclusive entertainment for city firms. Monypenny had acquired his wife, Hazel, much as he had acquired his career and his businesses, with a mixture of intuition and common sense but, mostly, with a canny eye on his own best interest. She was the daughter of a prominent local judge, well-groomed and well-educated, and worked as a research chemist at Heriot-Watt University. The Monypennys were always smart, dressed in the latest labels from Harvey Nicks, and seemed to continually preen themselves as if they were the sole attraction in the assembled company.

Sandy Kerr was an architect of some note, renowned for what had been called the 'stakeholder' approach to architectural design, which involved consulting a range of interested parties in a design project from the initial stages and developing the project through what was called 'negotiated progression' in an attempt to employ both harmonies and tensions in a positive way. A slim, inconspicuous man with an unruly mop of fair hair, he was happier dealing with queries regarding his own profession than he was rubbing his nose in committee politics.

Norman and Lucy Prentice were not, as it might have seemed at first, husband and wife, but brother and sister. He was a retired accountant who had been secretary of a firm that sold cavity wall fittings. She was the widow of a banker who had died prematurely and unexpectedly and she had, some years later, preferred to revert to her maiden name.

Rather grey and nondescript in character and appearance, the couple brightened up their quiet suburban lives by dedicating large amounts of time to a variety of good causes mostly associated with the arts.

Finally, there was Sir Herman Thombold, the legal advisor to the Association. Sir Herman was a large imposing man with well groomed grey hair and thick-rimmed black spectacles. He was dressed expensively and formally in a grey pinstripe suit and waistcoat. Herman Thombold had, for the best part of four decades, been one of Edinburgh's pre-eminent corporate solicitors and was prominent in the upper reaches of Edinburgh society.

After some preliminary niceties, the congregation gathered around the meeting table and Ord commenced the proceedings.

'Ladies and Gentlemen, this is an extraordinary meeting of the sub-committee with only one agenda item. Therefore, I shall ask Mrs McLaughlin to take a record of those attending, but we will not be considering the minutes of the last meeting.

'Neither will there be formal minutes of this meeting, but we will take notes which I will ask you to approve at the end. Now, for the substantive issue which we have to discuss, I welcome Sir Neville Thombold, whose reputation I'm sure, as they say, precedes him.' He nodded towards Thombold. 'Sir Neville…'

'Thank you, Chief Superintendent Ord. I'm pretty sure that you all have some inkling of the contents of the letter we'll be looking at.' He waved a folded piece of paper in the air. 'However, I'll try to give you the context as succinctly and as simply as possible.

'The Ballingall family, although not well-known to the public, have been major landowners in Edinburgh for three centuries. Their estate includes the notable gap site of Greenside Row at the bottom of Calton Hill. You may know from the press that a major development including a casino, several bars, a comedy club and a media centre has been proposed for the site. However, it now seems that such discussions may have been premature.' He paused to clear his throat.

'The senior member of the Ballingall family, Balfour Ballingall, died only six months ago. At the time of his death, he was resident in Canada. Before his death, which was not unexpected, he had taken some steps to resolve family business and lodged several papers with a Canadian lawyer, John Gilbert, who is, in fact, a second cousin and therefore a member of the Ballingall family himself. Included among the papers was this letter, which I shall now pass around the table before attempting to summarise the contents.' He took a folded sheet of paper from his inner jacket pocket and passed it to Lucy Prentice who was seated immediately to his right.

'As you will see from the letter, Balfour Ballingall considered himself a friend of the Playfair Association... '

Liz McLaughlin interrupted at this point, 'In fact, he was a long-term subscriber to our journal and had donated several sums over the years. The details are contained here.'

She brought out some loose papers and distributed them round the table with a satisfied smile, confident that she had demonstrated her thoroughness.

'Quite so.' Thombold looked a little peeved at the interruption. 'But if I could cut to the quick, so to say. Ignoring all the legal jargon, which, of course, I will endeavour to explain if required, the letter offers to sell the Greenside site to the Playfair Society for two million pounds on the understanding that it would be solely used for the provision of affordable social housing designed in accord with the vernacular architecture of the surrounding area.'

'Two million pounds?' enquired Lucy Prentice, 'Is that reasonable?'

'It's *nothing*, interjected Gordon Monypenny, 'merely a fraction of its true commercial value.'

'It seems like an outstanding opportunity,' said Sandy Kerr, Surely we must take advantage of it... ?'

'I agree, absolutely. I'm sure the City Council would welcome the opportunity to improve housing opportunities for the socially disadvantaged,' added Liz McLaughlin.

Ord raised a hand in a gesture intended to silence further contributions. I appreciate your thoughts and I'm sure everyone will have a full opportunity to air their views later. But I just want to clarify some issues before we discuss any action that we will recommend to the full committee. Firstly, the legal standing of this letter. Sir Neville?'

'Obviously I cannot predict any action that may follow through the courts or any other formal mechanism. I think it is possible, considering the substantial loss of assets that may arise from the transfer or sale indicated by the main clause contained within the said epistle, that other members of the Ballingall family may challenge the matter. Such a challenge may delay any conclusion for some time, perhaps a matter of years.' He paused to clear his throat. 'However, my fairly thorough investigation has failed to reveal any evidence that the document in question is not genuine. Indeed, Mr Gilbert has testified to receiving the letter personally from Balfour Ballingall and discussing his wishes with him. The senior Ballingall, before his death, had the legal right to dispose of the family assets as he wished. Provided that the letter is demonstrably genuine it is unlikely that any court or judicial# body would rule against his wishes.'

'You mean,' suggested Gordon Monypenny, 'that our claim could be challenged but that, eventually, we would be likely to get the land.'

'We cannot guarantee any conclusion until the proper legal process has been fulfilled, but that is a not unreasonable assumption predicated on the evidence currently available to us.

'There is another question we must consider,' suggested Ord. 'That is whether the Association would be in a position, constitutionally and financially, to purchase the land. Therefore, I asked Mrs McLaughlin, in anticipation of this meeting, to consult with Lord Buccleuch, the President of the Association, for some preliminary advice… Liz?'

'Obviously, any such matter would have to be taken by a full meeting of the Association, but his Lordship's initial view is positive. It would be unprecedented and probably inappropriate for the Association itself to own the project. We are not landowners or landlords. But a trust could be set up on behalf of the Association to manage the project to completion. The Association does not, of course, have a sum of money equivalent to that required, but his Lordship did not seem to think that that would be a problem… '

'I think I can say, based on my own financial experience,' said Norman Prentice, 'that there would be little difficulty in raising the necessary finance for the development of the scheme. The equity or collateral would easily serve to raise the necessary capital.'

'Ladies and Gentlemen,' Ord pre-empted any further

discussion. 'We have, I think, managed to outline the situation and everyone has had a chance to see the letter. What we have been asked to do is to formulate a recommendation to the annual general meeting of the Association. When everyone has had a chance to state their opinion we'll try to reach a consensus and nominate someone to write a report. But before that, I think a glass of wine may be in order and, as usual, the Association has generously provided some refreshments.'

They rose from the table. The letter was returned to Neville Thombold and he placed it in the corner of the blotter at his place on the table. Two bottles of wine were opened and glasses distributed among the company. General chatter ensued until, suddenly, there was a noisy clatter. A couple of glasses and a partially full bottle of wine had fallen from the table and smashed. Seemingly in attempting to prevent this, Hazel Monypenny had fallen to the ground.

Ord and Prentice helped her to her feet and, after a couple of minutes, the commotion had subsided. Then suddenly, everyone's attention turned to Sir Neville Thombold, who had noisily cleared his throat, staring at the table. 'The letter … it's gone!'

The next morning, Robert Ord was in Hamish McDavitt's flat in Regent Terrace relating the whole story

'It's a mystery right up your street, Hamish. The letter had just vanished into thin air, yet no-one could have left the room. After an initial search I took charge of the situation. The only alternative seemed to be to bring in some of my officers. Everyone had to be searched. Myself included, of course. It was a difficult decision to make, but I have to say that everyone, seeing the seriousness of the situation, immediately agreed

'And was anything found?'

'No, not a thing, Everything took until about midnight, but with no result. I slept on it but I'm no wiser this morning, It is impossible to explain what had happened. Therefore, Hamish, I came to see you, knowing you're something of a specialist in explaining the impossible?'

'Hmm.' Hamish rose from the settee and walked over to a framed print above the mantelpiece in his drawing room.

'It's strange that you should mention Gayfield House this morning, I've been there, of course, on Open Doors Day—to see the Barker panoramas. But here's another type of panorama, a print I acquired a few months ago.' He beckoned for Ord to join him. The print he indicated was a detailed view of the New Town and its environs looking down and over Calton Hill, seemingly from a great height.

'This is Thomas Dolby's view of Edinburgh sketched in 1870 from a hot air balloon suspended above the east end of Calton Hill. It is quite a spectacular view and it must have been a wonder in its time. The detail is impressive, there's a little steam train coming out of the tunnel at Scotland Street,and there's the old zoological gardens where tigers and bears were kept, just about at the bottom of Broughton Street as it is now. And yet there's something missing, round about this field here.' He pointed at the print.

Ord took a moment to trace the location that Hamish indicated.

'That's the site of Gayfield House itself!'

'Yes, and it was certainly there in 1875, as you know. But it's the only thing that Dolby seems to have missed from his plan. Now, there's a mystery for you!'

'Well… ' Ord mused over the matter, 'Maybe it was lost in the mist, or maybe it was being renovated and was too difficult to draw, or maybe Dolby had fallen out with the owner… '

'Or maybe', added Hamish, 'It was bewitched, like Major Weir's house that was said to disappear from view on nights when he was summoning the spirits.'

Ord, who was not in the mood for any frippery, gave a rueful look. 'You're not suggesting that there's something magic about the house and the disappearance of the letter?

'No, no. I'm sure there's a rational explanation for it, just as there is for Dolby's curious omission. Tell me more. I presume the search of the occupants of the room was thorough?'

'Absolutely, the best current practice was followed. Our men are fully trained, they have to deal with narcotics smugglers and suspect terrorists these days.'

'All hollow implements and clothes linings were investigated?'

'Oh yes: pens, watch-straps, Sir Neville's walking stick. All examined.'

'A piece of paper could be disguised as another piece of paper. Did you look into that.'

'Certainly, any letters, papers, even banknotes were passed through the x-ray machine.'

And, err… internal body… '

'Um, yes.' Ord clearly did not want to go any further into this than necessary. 'It was a category A search. The whole thing was a bit… '

'Uncomfortable', suggested Hamish.

Ord made a gesture that suggested Hamish was right.

'What about the contents of the room?'

'Every item was separately examined. And then every nook

and cranny was vacuumed and the contents examined. In fact here's the inventory and the photographs.'

Ord passed him a list and a couple of photographs of largely fluff and dirt against a sheet of white paper. Apart from dust and various fibres the list contained very little except common detritus: a cigarette end, a bent match, a piece of sticking plaster and a small plastic tag

Hamish inspected the list and the photographs carefully. 'Then, I suppose, you interviewed the members of the committee?'

'Yes, I did it myself in the presence of a senior officer Then I got the officer to question me. I didn't see much of consequence. I was standing by the table and I was distracted when the glasses toppled and Mrs Monypenny fell over trying to stop it. She had grazed her knee and broken the heel of her shoe. I helped her to her feet. Liz McLaughlin and the Prentices were nearby. They didn't remember anything of note except perhaps Lucy Prentice. She said something peculiar. That she was sure she felt a draught round about that time, as if a window had been opened. But we inspected the windows. They were all tightly screwed shut, hadn't been opened for months.'

'And what about the others?'

'Sandy Kerr and Gordon Monypenny were standing by the fireplace. Apparently, the accident had distracted both of them and Monypenny had nudged Kerr, spilling his drink over his tie. He seemed quite upset about the tie. Strange chap, but nothing useful to tell us.'

'And Sir Herman Thombold?'

'Well, that was odd. He was standing nearest the letter, at the table. But he claimed to have noticed nothing He seemed quite bemused by the whole thing. He even said that the letter could just as well have been spirited up the chimney!'

Hamish looked puzzled at this. 'I wouldn't have thought, he said, 'that the good Sir Herman was a devotee of the supernatural!'

Ord had a glance up at the Dolby print, for a moment he imagined he could see Gayfield House reappear and then disappear before his eyes.

'The truth is, Hamish, that we didn't really get anywhere. The fact of the matter is, the letter vanished. We don't know how or why, or where it is now. And it is a damned shame. We have nothing now to prove that the gap site was gifted to the Society!'

He shrugged. 'Is there anything else you would like to know?'

'Just one question', said Hamish. 'What sort of wine was being served?'

Ord knew that Hamish's oblique way of thinking about things could result in the most surprising and seemingly irrelevant questions, but he couldn't see the point this at all.

'Why, Bollinger—Grand Année, 1997, in fact. It seemed that the meeting might be the cause of something to celebrate!'

Hamish thought for a moment, screwing up his face as he sometimes did when pondering a mystery. Then, decisively, he headed for the door, reaching for his coat.

'You may have noticed that there is a slight drizzle, as there was last night. Nevertheless, I intend to take a short walk. Why don't you meet me at Gayfield House in, say one hour's time—and we'll see if we can solve this problem.'

Hamish had his walk. He headed down past the contentious Greenside site, then up past Rock House and the Scottish

Office building at the foot of Calton Hill with its monolithic columns and giant carved stone figures. Down by the Burns monument and eventually, down Croft-an-Righ by Holyrood Abbey and chapel and round by the Scottish Parliament and the Radical Road at the foot of Salisbury Crags. Exactly one hour later, having acquired one item, he was back at the entrance to Gayfield House.

They climbed the stairs and Ord unlocked the door and switched on the wall lights. The brightly lit room was set out as it had been the day before, the day of the incident. The chairs were set around the central table, some awry as they had been when the occupants had risen. The catering tables still contained a row of bottles and glasses, some broken, and the folded linen table clothes.

Hamish had a scout around, checking where each of the committee members had been at the time of the letter's disappearance. He seemed particularly interested in the marble fireplace and the large Chinese vase sat in the hearth.

'Bob,' he enquired, the contents of this jar were examined yesterday?'

'Absolutely, it was one of the first things we looked at.'

'Nevertheless, let's have another look. Can you give me a hand to lift it?'

They lifted the heavy ceramic vase on to the table and then, at Hamish's suggestion, tipped the contents on to the table. Surprisingly, there was a small mound of ash.

'Well, that certainly wasn't there yesterday, and the door has been locked ever since!'

'I know, but it is here now and I fear that if you examine this stuff you'll find it is the remnants of the letter—plus, I suspect, a little rubber.'

Ord's voice began to crack a little. 'But how could it burn. We confirmed that there was nothing inflammable in the room, and how could anything have happened in the locked room over the last twenty-four hours?'

'How can you have a fire without a flame? That's an interesting question. I thought about that for some time. But let me try to explain things one by one. Firstly, the strange impression of Lucy Prentice that there was a gust of air at the time of the disappearance struck me. We know that that was impossible as the windows were screwed fast. So, I thought, why should she have that impression? And when I had thought about it for a while, I realized that there could only have been one sequence of events—however bizarre it might seem!

Ord interjected, 'But Hazel Monypenny, she felt the same gust of air.'

'Well, yes, she said she had, but perhaps she had a reason to say so. Anyway, secondly, the contents of the room suggested something to me. Notably the bent matchstick and the little plastic tag. A tag, I think you'll find, identical to this one!'

Hamish took his hand out of his pocket and between his thumb and forefinger and displayed a small plastic tag,

Ord was mystified. 'It's the sort of thing you would get in a clothes shop, or a hundred other places.'

'Perhaps, but this one is attached to He opened his hand to show a small rubber balloon, ' …this?'

'A balloon? Ord was clearly confused.

'Indeed. Maybe it was the intrepid Thomas Dolby who gave me the idea. This is not, however, a hot air balloon like Dolby's. There is a little helium canister at the bottom and when you pull out the tag, Voila!' He did so, there was a little hiss and the balloon inflated. He let it go and it slowly rose to the ceiling

'I got this only a few hours ago from the office of City Days in Holyrood Road, Gordon Monypenny's corporate entertainment company. It's part of a pack of novelties they use on their outings.'

'And you're suggesting that this was used to facilitate the disappearance of the letter.'

'Yes, it was a very clever trick. It had to be enacted with perfect timing. Firstly, remember, I asked myself, why did Mrs Prentice claim to have felt a draught. Well, she didn't, but the memory can play strange tricks, particularly when we're distracted. Sometimes the senses get confused and one sense is substituted by another. It is sometimes called synaesthesia. Mrs Prentice actually heard the balloon inflating, a little later than she thought she had, but in the confusion *she thought* that she had actually felt the escaping air. Hazel Monypenny was quick to agree with her as it seemed to give another possible excuse for her little subterfuge with the glasses.'

'Mrs Monypenny was responsible for toppling the glasses?'

'Yes, remember I asked you what wine was served. Champagne. So the glasses were tall flutes, less stable than, say, red wine glasses. The bent matchstick, I suspect was employed. It's a little party trick. The glass is placed on a beer mat or the edge of a folded cloth, the bent match is placed under the edge of the base. The natural spring in the wood slowly straightens the match and the glass falls. But to make sure the effect was sufficiently dramatic, Hazel Monypenny pretended to try to catch the falling glass, thus exacerbating the commotion and distracting everyone's attention while also ensuring that the matchstick wasn't left in an obvious place.

Meantime, her husband had to carry out the harder part of the trick. Sandy Kerr was a little too close to him, so he used the fuss over the glasses falling to nudge him and spill his drink. Then, quickly, he grabs the letter, sticks it to the balloon with a little tack or tape, inflates the balloon and places it in the chimney where it rises as far as it can!'

'But how come it ended up in ashes in the Chinese vase? There's never been a fire in that grate.'

Hamish nodded slowly. 'How can be a fire without a flame? Well, remember that Hazel Monypenny worked in the chemistry department at Heriot-Watt University. I suspect what happened is this. The balloon would rise as far as it could in the chimney, well out of the range of the search conducted by your officers. But, of course, chimneys don't go straight up into the open air, or else rain and snow could come straight down. The balloon would rise as far as it could until it was stopped by the trap near the top. Remember that last night, like today, there was smirry rain around. I reckon that all the Monypennys had to do was smear the top of the balloon with some chemical, something like phosphorus I suppose that reacts with water. As soon as some moisture, even condensation, formed in the chimney top, it would catch fire and thus the pile of ashes at the bottom.'

Ord nodded, beginning to picture the incident. 'It's diabolically clever, but incredibly risky too. Anyone could have noticed.'

'Yes, I considered that. In normal circumstances no criminal would have taken such a preposterous risk. However, when I thought about it, I realised that they could afford to take the risk because, in the end, the stakes were not so high. If they had been caught in the act maybe they would have made it all out to be some sort of joke. Maybe they were just testing the security in the sub-committee. Anyway, what would they have done that was wrong. If the letter was still intact no harm would have been done, and, even now, what exact crime have they committed, and can we prove it? And, besides, they had some pretty significant support on the committee!'

'You mean they weren't the only ones involved?'

'Sir Herman Thombold knew where the letter was. He told us—it had 'been spirited up the chimney.' That was one of the first things I found odd about your story. It just seemed wrong to me. For a man like him, usually so measured in his expression, it seemed a remarkably colloquial, almost childlike thing to say. My granny used to say such things when I was a child. She'd hide a sweetie or a comic and pretend it was lost in the fire. She'd say 'it's awa up the lum' or 'the fairies have stolen it'. I couldn't imagine Thombold saying such a thing seriously, particularly in the circumstances. But then I thought of him saying it in an ironic way, with a sort of arrogant delight that the trick had succeeded. That he was smarter than the deluded fools who had fallen for it.'

'Then it was his idea?'

'It was probably at his insistence that the letter had to disappear, but it couldn't do so when in his possession. How would he explain that. The Monypennys probably came up with the plan, but they wouldn't have carried it out without some support. They have too good a conceit of themselves to initiate such a thing. But on the other hand they were fond of money, and there's no doubt that money is behind all this. Big business stood to lose a substantial sum if the letter were upheld. And who was most likely to have contact with the interested parties than a corporate solicitor. Thombold had placed the letter in the blotting pad, he was standing closest to it when it disappeared and, besides, I may be a cynic, but I've never heard of a solicitor, especially a very clever one like Sir Herman Thombold, losing anything to do with business unless they wanted to!'

Ord looked glum. 'Well, whatever we do there's no hope of reclaiming the letter. And without that there's not much chance of the Association taking over the gap site, despite Balfour Ballingall's wishes... and, as you say, it's not clear what crime has been committed, and, even if we can charge them our evidence might not hold water in a court of law!'

Hamish shook his head. 'Don't give up yet! I'm afraid this little case has moved out of the realm of police investigation into the realm of politics. Not my speciality. But you know people, Bob. There may be enough will on the part of Association to ensure that justice is done!'

'But Sir Herman and his cronies have a lot of power.'

'Unfortunately so', said Hamish. The world is weighed on the side of the unscrupulous. But we can fight back. We know people who are writers, artists, historians. The very fact that they have little money means that they have little to lose, but they do have the power of expression. Let's see if we can use that. And to start with, let's find a way to make it clear to Thombold and the Monypennys that we're wise to their little trick!'

'I'll look forward to seeing their faces when they realise, said Ord.

'Meanwhile', said Hamish, 'let's get out of here. Perhaps we can treat ourselves to a wee dram at the Barony Bar and try to trace any remains of the old Edinburgh Zoo.'

THE SPECTATOR AT THE HIPPODROME

It was one Saturday afternoon in late Spring when Hamish McDavitt found himself in the Forresthill Bar in Forrest Road. He liked coming here on weekend afternoons when the local musicians gathered and played a variety of Scottish traditional tunes. In the evenings the younger musicians came in. They were technically perfect and accomplished, but the older folk, led by Ewan Grant, a little very whiskered old man who played the 'moothie'—also known as the mouth organ or harmonica—played the way that Hamish preferred—rough and ready, stopping and starting a little and not always exactly in concert but genuine and heartfelt. For centuries Scots had made their own entertainment like this, in bothies, crofts, single-ends, wherever they could gather together. Today was an exceptionally convivial day-little shafts of sunlight gleaming through the windows as small knots of customers downed a beer or a dram to a background of jigs and reels: *The Four-poster Bed*, *My Love is but a Lassie Yet* and *The Hen's March to the Midden*.

Hamish also liked, on these occasions, to have a Lagavulin, a tangy and slightly bitter malt but with a surprisingly smooth and lingering aftertaste redolent of burning peat and lichen and moss covered drystane dykes, or occasionally, a Tomatin, a slightly fusty Speyside malt with suggestions of old school desks, chalk and leathery tawse.

He always dedicated his first dram to Seumas Gunn, his old friend, now deceased—a poet and singer of some renown, whose bust in bronze was preserved on the shelf behind the bar, always accompanied by a bottle of Lagavulin, kept almost, but not quite empty—in case Seamus was thirsty.

Charlie Hog was behind the bar pouring beer for a new influx of customers.

'Busy today', Hamish enquired.

'Not bad', replied Charlie, 'considering that I didn't open until half-past-two.'

'Half-past-two? Why was that?'

'Well, didn't the clocks go forward last night. But I got confused and put mine *backwards*! I was two hours too late!'

This this afternoon, Hamish was in the company of his friends—Tam Wauch and Keith Baxter. Tam was Professor of Human Geography and Keith was Chief Librarian for the Humanities at the University of Edinburgh.

They were often delightful company but were amongst the most pedantic people that Hamish had ever known, pursuing a topic until they had exhausted every possible avenue.

On this occasion they were avidly discussing the topography of Edinburgh Castle in light of recent studies of entrenchment, battlements and defensive formations.

Tam held the view that the Castle was systematically planned according to a mathematical formula to avoid blind spots that could be used by invaders. Keith, on the other hand, thought that, although the battlements were carefully planned, such an arrangement was also a consequence of the unique topography of the Castle Rock.

They were interrupted in this fascinating discourse when a

good friend of Hamish came into the bar.

Hamish signalled for him to come over to where they were standing, at the back of the bar beside the arched partition with the Heart of Midlothian pendants.

'This is Detective Inspector Nigel Stonelaw.' Hamish introduced him. 'I'm surprised to see you here, Nigel, a bit off your usual track!' Hamish knew that Stonelaw was more usually found around the corner in the Bow Bar in Victoria Street, where there was a wide selection of real ales. What brings you to these parts?'

Stonelaw looked back and forward at Hamish and his companions as if deciding whether to trust them with a confidence. 'Well... actually I've just been at the University round the corner. Hush hush business, of course.'

Hamish and his friends took on a serious complexion and moved a little closer together. 'I'm sure, however,' said Hamish, 'that if you wish to discuss it, nothing will go outside these walls.' And he nodded slightly to Tam and Keith.

Stonelaw squirmed a little as if slightly uncomfortable, but then he also nodded, as if contented. Hamish had ascertained, correctly, that he had something to get off his chest.

'Of course, this is strictly off the record, but, in an official capacity... He emphasised the word 'official', ' ...in an official capacity, I was asked to visit the Department of Parapsychology.'

'I know it well,' said Keith, 'they have a large library budget but not much to spend it on and they only have a couple of months until the end of the University financial year.'

'But no doubt they'll have had a *premonition* of that!' interjected Tam, who had scant regard for the University's venture into esoteric areas.

'Anyway,' Stonelaw continued, 'we had been approached by them. Apparently, it's all the rage in the States, mediums and that sort of thing supporting the official investigations of the police. I was sent to see what I thought.' Stonelaw hesitated.

'Thought it was a lot of nonsense at first, but I have to say, I've been pretty impressed by what I've seen today'

'You had better tell us about it then,' said Hamish.

Stonelaw related his tale.

'I went to visit Professor Roger Pinney, an American who occupies the Arthur Koestler Memorial Chair at the University. He was very welcoming but got to the point pretty quickly.

'Inspector, you want a demonstration of our abilities, I can see. You are a sceptic, but I suppose that is your nature as a police officer. I'll do what I can to show you what I do. I can't say whether you'll be satisfied or not.'

'OK, then,' I said. 'Show me what you do. I'll keep an open mind. That's what detectives are trained to do.'

'Let's try something quite simple. Inspector, could you write down for me some personal details say your date of birth.'

'So I did that, on a pad of paper he presented to me.

"Right,' he said to his secretary, 'suppose you get the local telephone directory.'

'And then he asked me to open the directory at the page corresponding to the year I was born—'51—and to read down to the line corresponding to the month I was born—the eleventh line, for November. I was to read the entry carefully to myself and concentrate on it.

'And, amazingly, after thinking for a minute or so, he was able to tell me exactly what it was. I've taken a note of it here in my book. He took a little black notebook from his pocket. 'Joseph Bailey, 127 Craigmount Brae, 339 16757.'

'I was surprised, but then I thought about it. 'Wait a minute,' I said, 'I've seen a television documentary about people who can do this sort of thing—savants, they call them?'

"I'm flattered, Inspector,' he replied, 'that you think I can memorise about half a million names, addresses and telephone numbers. That would be truly remarkable. But honestly, it is much easier to read your mind!' Then he came up with something else. 'But let's try a slightly more advanced experiment,' he said. He took from his drawer a blindfold and a pair of ear plugs. 'We often use these, not only does it gainsay any accusations of cheating, but, by cutting out the outside world it also helps us to concentrate.' He put on the blindfold and ear plugs and also picked up a note pad and pencil.

'Then he continued. 'Now what I'd like you to do is go to the telephone and phone Mr Bailey. Apologise for disturbing him at this time in the morning. If we can't get him we'll choose someone else from the list. Then could you ask him simply to think of an object in his house and think hard about it. Meanwhile. I'll try to portray it on this paper.'

'Well, you'll never guess. The object he drew was exactly the object that Mr Bailey thought of—a clock! I was nonplussed.

'I stared at the drawing then the clock on the office wall. They were identical except that in the drawing the hands of the clock were set one hour earlier than the hands of the clock on the wall.'

There was a silence for a moment as the musicians launched into a vigorous rendition of the hornpipe *Harvest Home*.

'Ah, remember that it was the spring solstice yesterday,' Tam suddenly said, 'Mr Bailey had clearly forgotten to move his clock one hour forward!' There was a pause while the company took in this additional extraordinary point.

Eventually, Stonelaw nodded in appreciation of this observation and also in a fashion that was meant to suggest that he'd related something extraordinary. 'And that's it, Hamish. Pretty impressive, eh?'

'Umm… ' Hamish pondered. 'Just let me take a minute to wash my hands.'

A few minutes later Hamish returned. 'OK,' Hamish said, 'let's try a similar experiment, then, but right here! Keith, will you get the Edinburgh and Lothians Post Office Directory from the shelf at the back of the pub. Now, Nigel, write down, say, the day and the month of your birthday here.'

Stonelaw, as requested, wrote down on the back of a beer mat the numbers '23' and '11'. Meanwhile, Keith had retrieved a rather tatty thick telephone directory from the back shelf.

'Now,' he said, 'Nigel, will you go to page number eleven of the directory and scroll down to the twenty-third line and concentrate on what it says.'

Hamish raised his hands to his temples as if concentrating very hard.

After about thirty seconds he said, 'I think I can see it now —Anderson, Mrs Anderson… now, the initial—N, I think…'

'No, but very close.'

'Ah, M… Mrs Marion Anderson.'

'Well it just says M here, but I suppose you're right. That's quite… amazing… ' Inspector Stonelaw raised his head from the directory to see that Tam still looked puzzled but that Hamish and Keith were grinning broadly at him.

'Wait a minute, it's a trick isn't it.' He stared at his beer and then at the beer mat as if thinking very hard.

'Och,' said Keith, 'we knew it would be a trick if Hamish

was involved. Can't say I know how he did it though.'

Stonelaw furrowed his brow then suddenly started. 'I know. I'd already told you the month, hadn't I! It must be something to do with that!'

'Yes,' said Hamish, you're getting the idea. 'It's quite a simple trick really, but in essence the same as the trick employed by the ingenious Professor Pinney.'

'You're right, I already knew the month, so it wasn't too hard, when I was at the lavatory, to have a quick glance at page eleven. Obviously, also, the day had to be between one and thirty-one. Therefore, I only looked at lines one to thirty-one. These were all, conveniently, 'Anderson'. I didn't quite have time to get it absolutely off pat, therefore the confusion between M and N. 'Marion' was just my little invention since the directory usually only has initials. It was the icing on the cake, so to speak. But it almost fooled you, didn't it?'

'Hold on, however,' said Stonelaw, 'Pinney didn't know anything about my birth date, and what about all that business with the clock?'

'I agree,' said Hamish, but Pinney had more than a few seconds to prepare it, and he's a professional. This particular device had probably been set up for some time and he probably had other little tricks, involving gazetteers or catalogues for example.

'What he does is very similar to what stage magicians do, to distract you from what he is actually doing. The whole thing about numbers is just hokum. There may be half a million numbers in the book, but exactly how many combinations does he have to remember? Anyone who is likely to be the subject of this test will be say, between 25 and 55. So that is thirty possible pages, and twelve lines per page to memorise.

Not a difficult task for someone trained in mnemonic techniques.'

'But what about the drawing of the clock and all that? How can that be a trick.'

'Well, that is a bit more difficult, and I can't say that I can explain it exactly, But let's take an educated guess.'

'We've already agreed that what he has done is quite feasible through memorising about three hundred telephone directory entries, and this trick itself is probably enough to sufficiently impress most people. But Pinney is a complete professional. He has to continually develop his techniques.

'Now, we've already narrowed the scope of the trick down to a limited number of entries, but perhaps we can cut it down a bit more—some months are more common for births than others—or perhaps he has chosen a sample at random. Or perhaps it is a convenient selection, old folk who are likely to have been at home at the time they might be phoned. So, when Pinney has completed his little memory trick, he could stop there, but now, by chance, he has an extra card up his sleeve, so to say. He remembers that Mr Joseph Bailey is one of his primed candidates. He now has one extra illusion to convince you that it wasn't a trick after all but a paranormal talent.'

'But how would he know that they would choose a clock?'

'I don't know. Maybe he had circulated these people and convinced them that they were entered for some kind of competition that required them to answer a set question.

'Some older people might have been regarded as more susceptible to this. Or maybe there was some sort of technique of suggestion. Hypnotists and illusionists do that sort of thing all the time. Anyway, the clock was an easy item to draw and, one final little touch, the hour was an hour early. You had no way of checking that, did you. But it served the purpose of distracting you from questioning what was happening—the suspension of disbelief I believe it is called.'

Then Hamish suddenly broke out into a little chuckle. 'In fact, when I think of it, perhaps Mr Bailey wasn't primed at all! Perhaps it was obvious that the day after changing all the clocks in his house that that object would instantly spring to mind!'

'But,' said Tam, 'That can't be right. Mr Bailey had forgotten to put his clock forward.'

'Hmm...' thought Hamish.

'Ah,' interjected Keith, 'didn't Pinney ask you to mention the time of the morning to him!'

'Of course, and naturally, he would look at his clock!'

'And,' added Hamish, 'we only have Pinney's drawing to suggest that his clock looked like that anyway!'

Stonelaw was still gazing at the clock above the bar and the musicians were grinding out a sonorous version of *Leaving Lismore* when Charlie Hog came over to Hamish and handed him a twenty pound note and a slip of paper. Your first winner from the Cheltenham Festival. Second Sight in the 3.30.'

Stonelaw looked at Hamish, 'second sight?'

'Just coincidence.' Hamish smiled. 'Never underestimate coincidence. Arthur Koestler was not a very nice man but an interesting writer. He had a theory that probability was only true in a limited sphere. Just as Einstein showed in the theory of relativity that time was only constant in the observable world, Koestler suggested that probability only functioned within our limited observations of the world. Another well-known writer wrote a piece called *The Spectator*

135

at the Hippodrome. He imagines a crowd at a horse race. The ordinary punter—like most of us—is only intent on part of the race—perhaps focusing only on the horse he has bet on. Someone else, say a steward or a judge, might be watching from a more elevated viewpoint, trying to concentrate on the race as a whole. Finally, he imagines some else—someone omniscient—who sees not only every horse in the race, but every race and every spectator all at once!'

Tam laughed. 'And is that how you foxed the bookies, Hamish?'

'No, unfortunately bookmakers only work in a very limited world indeed.' He looked at Stonelaw. 'I don't rely on any hocus pocus, and I don't advise you to either. If I want to pick a horse, I look at the tipsters in the *Sporting Daily.* If I want to know about geography I would ask you, Tam. If I wanted to know about police procedure I would ask you, Nigel, but there is nothing much for which I would rely on the ingenious Professor Pinney!'

They shared a laugh while Tam launched into a little tirade about the University and the gullibility of its senior officers when faced with new trends and fads and the music plodded away in the background.

'Well, enough of that,' said Keith, after a little while, 'I'm looking at the Malt of the Moment board and I'm picturing something in a glass, something smooth with just a hint of peat and spring water. I hope that you can read my mind! Double Macallans all round please, Charlie.'

THE PREMATURE DEATH OF THE BEAUTIFUL GRACE BONNINGTON

Hamish McDavitt and his good friend Tam Wauch were seated in the upstairs restaurant of Valvona and Crolla in Elm Row, a long established eaterie to which they would adjourn occasionally for a special treat. Valvona and Crolla was legendary amongst Edinburgh foodies. In the downstairs shop there was a cornucopia of focaccio, prosciutto, chorizo and paesano sausage. Hams, cheeses and breads to suit all tastes—including the more exotic ewe's milk cheeses, salami stuffed with fennel seeds, or a brioche made with chocolate, sultanas and vanilla butter. Today, Hamish had ordered vongole al forno con pancetta—cherry stone clams with lemon sauce and Tam had chosen zampone con polenta e Lenticche—stuffed pig's trotter with polenta and lentils.

'Why don't we try the adriana langhe chardonnay?' Hamish suggested. 'It has a bouquet of acacia flowers, citrus fruits, hazelnuts and honey.'

'I didn't know you were a connoisseur of fine wines,' said Tam.

'I'm not,' said Hamish, 'That's why I'm reading from the menu!'

After they had exhausted their discussion of the day's menu and the wonderful range of comestibles to be sampled downstairs, their attention turned to the main feature of the day in the *Daily Scot*.

'It's a strange affair,' Tam said, 'just about everyone had forgotten about the Bonningtons, then this happens.'

What had happened was that one of Scotland's richest women, Deidre Love, née Bonnington, had passed away in her estate in East Lothian. She was only a week short of her one hundredth birthday and had lived a reclusive life of many years. This would normally have only merited a short but decent obituary in the *Daily Scot*, probably from a stock of such that had been accumulated over a period of years, but the circumstances were unusual. In fact, Deidre Love had been the cause of her own death, consuming a fatal dose of a prescription drug that she took for a minor heart condition while her full-time nurse had been shopping She was discovered in her bed at around noon, clutching an old picture of her only sister, Grace, who had died at a tragically young age. To further complicate the issue, the family library, containing all the papers of the Bonnington and Love families, had been set alight and all its papers, books and memorabilia destroyed. It was presumed that this could only have been the work of Deidre herself. Subsequently, it was discovered that she had recently drawn up a will that left around half her estate to various charities and the rest divided between the family of the nanny who had cared for her as a child and the nurse who had attended her in her last years.

The unusual nature of these events had led the papers to reconstruct some of the career of the Bonnington sisters and their tragic history.

Deidre Bonnington and her sister Grace, younger than Deidre by one year, had been noted socialites in the thirties. Born to a middle-class family in Riccarton, they had benefited from a broad education and a great deal of travel as their father was a graded diplomatic officer stationed in several commonwealth offices. The sisters were of an adventurous nature and became known for their pioneering interest in aviation. Flying was all the rage in the early thirties and female aviatrices such as Neta Snook and Amelia Earhart were great celebrities and often in the popular press. The Bonnington sisters were doted on by their father subsequent to the premature death of their mother in the late twenties and, since he had inherited a substantial estate in Sutherland, he could afford to indulge their interests. He purchased a Kinner Canary biplane which flew from East Fortune airfield. Sightings of the sisters flying over Edinburgh in the bright yellow 'canary' were a talking point of the time.

Grace was the beauty of the two, slim with flowing golden locks. Deidre was plainer and stockier, with shoulder length, unkempt dark hair and a boyish demeanour. The photo that graced the front page of the *Daily Scot* showed these differences, featuring them together, as they always were, in front of a Lockheed Vega along with Jerry Love, the American entrepreneur whom Deidre had sensationally married at the age of only twenty two.

'Sensationally' because it was the beautiful Grace who attracted all the attention at that time. She had a string of connections with moneyed and titled young men and the cream of attractive bachelors on the social rounds of the time. But all were short-lived and often tempestuous. Then Deidre, the more serious and introspective of the two, had suddenly announced that she was to be married. To an older man who, apart from his other attributes, was massively wealthy—Jerry Love, the owner of the American Love Aviation Company which had pioneered the development of early passenger aircraft such as Vega and Orion

Tam was looking at the photograph in the newspaper, which was juxtaposed with another, a studio photo of the young Grace Bonnington which was supposedly, the one that Deirdre had held in her hand for her last moments on earth.

'Old photographs have this curious appeal. Who was it that said that photographs all have a feel of death about them, because the moment they represent is lost and can never be retrieved? Here they are, smiling and so young and happy, not knowing what was to happen to them!'

And indeed, something very tragic had happened. Firstly, their father had died and there had been reportedly, some difficulty in the disposition of the estate. Then, when this had been resolved, one year after Deirdre's marriage, Love, Deidre and Grace had all decamped to a small town near Adelaide in Australia where conditions, apparently, were ideal for flying and where they planned to develop an aeroplane to provide fast and efficient transportation around Australasia and the Pacific islands.

One day, when the maintenance crew were stocking up with provisions, Love had decided to take his sister-in-law Grace for a short flight. Unfortunately, a fuel hose was leaking. The plane exploded on the runway, killing them both instantly. Deidre, who was standing nearby, was also injured and took some time to recover. After this she never remarried, settled at her estate near East Fortune in Scotland and devoted her time to promoting aviation and various good causes. It was said that she would tolerate no visitors—not even the old nanny who had raised the sisters as children. Eventually she had faded from the public eye-until now.

'It's a straightforward enough story, although tragic,' said

Tam, 'but perplexing. It might not seem infeasible for an old infirm woman to end her own life if she was in severe pain or distress. But there was no evidence that Deidre Love was any more of an invalid than before. And the timing—just before her hundredth birthday. It doesn't really make sense. And then destroying all the family documents and memorabilia! Why!'

Hamish appeared to be unusually contemplative as he munched the last of his clams. 'Tam', he said, 'It is a very peculiar case and hard to make sense of. I can't help but think that there is a clue in the photograph—you suggested it yourself, the uncanny nature of a moment frozen in time. We presume that Deidre kept it as a nostalgic evocation of the past and yet she held on to it while, at the same time, we presume, deliberately destroying all the record that remained of herself and her family.'

Hamish picked up the newspaper and perused the two photos of the sisters for some time.

At last he said, 'I'm reminded of the famous garden of forking paths. It sees our lives as little stories of a sort. At certain junctures we make choices and our own story forks one way or the other. If you think about it, just as our own lives have done. You, Tam, had your own choice to make a few years ago. I have also had my own decisions to make, as we all have, even in a life that seems, outwardly, to have run smoothly. A wise man, probably wiser than you or I, learns to have no regrets about the path he chooses because he can't know what the alternatives would have been! I believe that there is a very clever movie, set in a subway, that explores this problem!'

'But did the Bonningtons have any choices to make. Their lives were marked by an unusual tragedy which they couldn't prevent.'

Hamish shifted, almost uneasily, as he stared for a moment at his empty plate.

'Tam, you have already said yourself that the story of the Bonnington sisters doesn't seem complete or explicable now that we have the latest news, even if it is only partial. However... He paused and concentrated for a moment as if gazing at something in the distance. However, I could tell you another story, it might be true or might simply be a product of my imagination. It is a very sad story.'

Tam stared at him. The tone of Hamish's had changed and seemed altogether more serious than before.

'If you like,' said Hamish, 'I will tell you this alternative story?'

Tam looked at Hamish and nodded. He knew Hamish could joke about the things he sometimes saw—things beyond the ken of ordinary folk. But he knew when Hamish was serious. He remembered how he had helped him through his own crisis some years ago.

Hamish poured another glass of chardonnay and commenced his story, He told it in a hushed and measured voice, as if relating a shared personal secret.

'All those years ago in Australia, we are led to believe that Jerry Love intended to take his sister-in-law on the fatal flight and that, in consequence, they were both killed instantaneously in a tragic explosion. I am presuming that it was, of course, an accident, rather than a deliberate act of murder!'

'But surely,' Tam interjected, 'Deidre would have no reason to murder her new husband and her sister, to whom she was obviously devoted.'

'No, Deirdre wouldn't have done that, even if she had had

the opportunity. It isn't Deirdre I'm thinking of. It's Grace. From all accounts she was a flirty, capricious and inconsistent thing, jealous of her older sister, but not a murderer, I think.

'However, from what we know, she loved her freedom, the flying, the adventure. She liked men, perhaps, but not enough to tie herself to one, to become just another pretty wife for an up-and-coming young businessman!

'No, Grace wasn't that type, despite what everyone thought, she was much deeper than her sister. Perhaps she felt many conflicting emotions—not uncommon when siblings are so close together—or perhaps the problem was that she found it hard to feel emotions or empathy at all. That is sometimes why people choose to live alone. Hamish hesitated. ' …But I've neglected my story. Let me get back to it… '

He took a small sip of wine and put the glass down slowly, his eyes a little screwed up as if trying to imagine something that only remained as a half image.

'Suppose… just suppose, that on that day—perhaps the weather was fine or there was an unusual cloud formation—Love had decided to fly. But suppose, as actually seems more likely when you think about it, that he wanted to take not Grace, his sister-in-law, but Deirdre, his wife, on the flight!

'Now the explosion occurs. It is an accident, I believe. But Grace Bonnington is weak. Perhaps she is not clever in the conventional way, but she thinks quickly, as a pilot is trained to do. She realises that she is left alone. She has never been apart from her sister. What will happen to her life now. And what will happen to the Love Corporation inheritance now her sister is dead? There may have been various provisions, and Grace will surely know of them—and, suppose, just suppose, that she also knows that her father's provision for the sisters

143

has not, perhaps, realised as much as they had hoped.

'As I say, she is weak and, despite her beauty, has always envied her sister's success and easy way with people compared to her own awkwardness. So, perhaps, she hasn't been hurt by the explosion, but she can rub dirt into her hair and feign injury. The period of recovery and prolonged grieving will give her enough time to carry out her plan.'

Hamish hesitated. Tam had taken out the *Daily Scot* and was gazing intently on the little picture of the beautiful and fêted Miss Grace Bonnington.

'You see, a photograph endures but the signifiers of beauty are themselves often fickle. The golden locks can be cropped and dyed. The bright white teeth darkened and chipped, the svelte figure lost through an injudicious diet. And even, the face itself. The nose can be broken, bloodied and bruised. And what would it require to do such a thing? Determination self hatred… courage? Now she realises that she is alone. She cannot risk meeting anyone who may see through her deception, such as the nanny who raised her as a child.

'So, according to my story, Grace Bonnington becomes Deirdre Love, inheritor of the Love Corporation fortune, and since then many years have passed. Who knows what dark thoughts, regrets, or memories went through her head since then until… until the forthcoming one hundredth birthday. Not a cause for celebration but for panic! The media will resurrect the story. Perhaps a book will be written.

'She cannot face the possibility of exposure, so she takes the necessary steps, destroying the family papers and all possible evidence on the way. The only possession she keeps is the photograph, not of her sister but herself, a memory of what might have been.'

Hamish looked up Tam had been rapt in thrall to his story, but now his face looked aghast, at the contemplation, perhaps, of a final death—an ending to the story.

'Of course,' said Hamish, 'this is just a story, constructed by myself. It is only one of an infinity of forking paths.'

'But… ' Tam hesitated, 'it is possibly the only story that fits all the facts and fully explains the nature of the death of… of whoever died that day!' He was silent for a moment.

'What will happen now?'

'Nothing, of course. No one else knows this alternative tale of the Bonnington sisters—except, perhaps, the nurse who was with her in the last days, and she has been well provided for. Either Deirdre or Grace will have their last wish, that the Bonnington sisters are dead and gone and their only record is in a couple of old photographs that recalls an occasion when they were as happy as they ever would be.' Hamish drained the last dregs of his glass of wine.

'Often the past is easier to contemplate than the present. It is something we all have to bear sometimes.'

Tam ordered another bottle of chardonnay to finish their lunch, but a contemplative darkness had set over the occasion which was not dispelled. Sometimes, thought Hamish, however difficult it is to encounter a death or a tragedy elsewhere, it mostly serves to remind us of ourselves and the fragile life of forking paths that we all lead.

THE BLACK REDEEMER

Two or three times a week Louie Delamonte would leave his flat in Scotland Street and wander sound the corner to the Cumberland Bar for a constitutional half and a half pint. He generally preferred doing so in the winter months when the bar was comparatively quiet or in the middle of the summer when it was mercifully free of the numerous students who frequented it during university term-time. The Cumberland Bar, in fact, was well known for the English home counties crowd who used it as their base. Many of the better-off English students, who could afford something more substantial than the various halls of residence dotted around the city lived in nearby flats on the northern edge of the New Town.

On this particular day in early summer the bar was busy with businessmen out for lunch and with a spattering of students celebrating the end term. Louie was rather squeezed on a stool by the edge of the bar near the window.

He was particularly annoyed by a couple of young men whose elbows occasionally nudged him. He couldn't help but hear snatches of their conversation. One had the sort of plummy southern voice that Louie didn't care for. The other a flat rather monotonous voice of uncertain origin. From what he could gather, the English one was rather boastfully discoursing on two themes: the successful conclusion of his exams at Edinburgh University and the flat that he owned but shared with other students at 24 Cumberland Street. Louie was, with difficulty, trying to ignore this conversation and concentrate on the *Daily Scot*, when he caught a few words from the second of the men, whose back was turned from him and his head silhouetted against the sun coming in the window. Twice, in a rather urgent tone he seemed to say, 'The black redeemer... the black redeemer... ' In the way that sometimes odd things that you observe or overhear puzzle or perplex you, Louie wondered what this strange statement could possibly mean, He looked up and examined the two men. He was surprised to see that the confident young Englishman, who was facing him, suddenly appeared to be quite crestfallen and anxious!

Louie had quite forgotten about this until the very next day when, standing at the very same spot in the bar, he opened the *Daily Scot* and saw the headline. 'Student Brutally Murdered at 24 Cumberland Street.' Immediately, he decided that he should phone his friend Hamish McDavitt.

Nigel Stonelaw was walking round from the police station at Gayfield Square to the murder scene in Cumberland Street that same day when he received a call on his mobile from Hamish McDavitt. When he heard that Hamish perhaps had some information on the case in question, he immediately invited him to join him at the scene of the crime, which was only a short stroll from Hamish's flat on Royal Terrace. 'I don't know too much about it myself,' Stonelaw said. 'I was up late last night investigating a supposed drug drop at a Lothian Road nightspot involving a well-known local footballer. In the end, nothing transpired. When I got in at about lunchtime, I was given the details. The night shift had already investigated the scene quite thoroughly.'

They were now inside the flat at 24 Cumberland Street. It had been cordoned off in the usual way. Stonelaw took Hamish into the study in which the murder had been committed. There was a desk and chair and not much else in the room. The desktop had been cleared and the only indication left that a violent murder had taken place was a dark stain on the carpet.

The victim was a young Englishman—name of Piers Campbell-Hawes. He was a second-year chemistry student at the University. Owned this flat, apparently, although it was bought for him by his parents. They live in Crondall, Surrey, and his father's something big in a City investment bank. He shared the flat with two other students.'

'And he was sitting at this desk when he was murdered?' asked Hamish.

'Yes, fatal trauma. Very sudden. A blow to the back of the head with a hammer or a similar blunt instrument. No murder weapon discovered on the scene. It's not clear whether he knew the assailant or whether the assailant crept up behind him. The door to the study was open and the front door unlocked.

Hamish examined the desk and chair. The desk faced the window at a slight angle. The chair was a conventional padded swivel chair on wheels. 'How was the body discovered?' he asked.

'By one of his flatmates, Gillian Martins, a final year English student at the University, from Linlithgow. She had just finished her finals and was at a party with fellow students at the Teviot Row Union. She returned at about 3.00am, saw the light in the study and found him there slumped over the desk. He had been dead for some time. We estimate the time of death at between 7.30pm and 8.30pm.'

'Hmm,' said Hamish. 'That means, I suppose, that Gillian Martins had a watertight alibi.'

'Oh yes. We checked that out as per usual. Seemed an unlikely suspect, however. She was extremely upset. Apparently, she and Campbell-Hawes had been attached... romantically attached... for a couple of months.'

'And what about the other flatmate?'

'That's another Scottish student, studying computer science. His name's Scott Pride, from Grangemouth; bright lad, won a bursary to Heriots. Not from a very well-off family but, by all accounts, as I've said, very clever—top of his year and all that.

'And does he have an alibi?'

'Yes, absolutely sound. He was, in fact, sitting the last of his exams in computer science, up at King's Buildings. The exam lasted from 7.00pm to 9.00pm—apparently they have them in the evening and at weekends now, especially if they need dedicated workshops, in order to use the space efficiently. He even showed us the transcript from the exam. It was marked by the computer itself. It indicates that he was logged on from 7.00pm until 9.00pm. Did rather well. Got 96%. Then he went to the McEwan's Alehouse with his classmates. Got quite drunk by all accounts and didn't come home at all that night. Kipped on the floor with a friend in South Clerk Street.'

Hamish looked thoughtful. 'So,' he said, both Campbell Hawes's flatmates were out celebrating when, we presume, he was still at home studying?'

'No, Hamish, surprisingly you're wrong there. In fact, Campbell-Hawes has already finished his exams and had been out at a party the night before. Apparently, he had decided on a quiet night at home to recover.'

Hamish frowned. 'I'm a little perplexed, then. If he wasn't studying, why was he sitting at his desk?'

'Aha, I wondered when you would get round to that. In fact, that is one of the most intriguing parts of the case. He was playing chess!'

'Playing chess. On his own?'

'No, against his computer! Forensics have taken it away for examination. But they've already given me a couple of printouts from the screen.' He took two pieces of folded paper from his inside jacket pocket. This,' he said, 'pointing at one, 'is the position of the chess game that he had just finished. And this,' he waved the other piece of paper quite flamboyantly towards Hamish, 'is an email message that had popped up on the screen! Unfortunately, the lab boys don't think we'll be able to trace it. It had been encrypted or re-routed or something.'

Hamish took the piece of paper from Stonelaw. The message on it was short and quite explicit: 'Game Over. You Lose. You're Dead. Goodbye. The Black Redeemer.'

At around 5.00pm that evening, Nigel Stonelaw was seated in the interview room at Gayfield Square police station. He had, as Hamish suggested, spoken to Louie Delamonte who had immediately identified the English student he had overheard in the bar as Piers Campbell-Hawes, As regards the other person he had overheard, few details were forthcoming. He hadn't seen his face. All he could remember was that he was dressed casually, in a leather jacket with turned up sleeves and a baseball cap. Hamish had, quite surprisingly, taken an interest in the diagram of the chess game from the computer.

'Didn't know you were a student of the game,' said Stonelaw.

I'm not,' replied Hamish, 'but I know someone who is, and, if you'll excuse me, I'm going off to find him.'

While Hamish was away, Stonelaw waited to interview the two flatmates. They had both given brief statements to police officers and had been given time to return to their parents' houses and get over the initial shock. They had agreed to return to be interviewed that evening

First, Stonelaw spoke to Gillian Martins. She was a prettyish slim girl with long blonde hair. Her lips were rouged, but her face was drawn and tired-looking, Her mascara had run a little. She puffed nervously on a cigarette.

'Miss Martins, could you tell me how long you had known Mr Campbell-Hawes?'

'Since the beginning of second year, I suppose. Piers's parents had bought the flat in Cumberland Street for him, although I suppose it was really an investment for them. He was looking for a couple of flatmates. My parents had met his parents on holiday in Madeira so that's how we got in touch. I moved in right away, then Scott moved in a bit later.'

'And you were very fond of Mr Campbell-Hawes?'

She hesitated for a moment and bit her lip. 'We'd been going together for about two months …I …I don't know exactly. He was going to take me down to Surrey sometime in the summer. We hadn't arranged a date or anything like that.' She stopped for a minute and gulped, her face creasing a little. 'His parents had a yacht… He said we'd go sailing, maybe to the Isle of Wight… '

Relaying all this information had taken something out of the girl, so Stonelaw gave her a few moments to recover.

'Miss Martins,' he said, 'do you have any idea at all who might have wanted to murder your boyfriend?'

She shook her head.

'What about Mr Pride. Did he get on with you both?'

'Oh, Scott. I don't know. He was OK but he was a geek really. I don't know if he had any real friends, just computers. I don't really know why Piers took him in. But he was alright I suppose. He kept the place tidy and never made a fuss. Sometimes I thought he gave me strange looks but... '

'And there was no-one else that might have borne him a grudge?

'No.' She shook her head. Then she reflected for a moment. 'But he had some new friends at the chess club the Edinburgh Chess Club. I never met them, but I thought they were maybe weird. Piers didn't seem to know whether he liked them or not. But he was quite keen. It was his new hobby. I thought it was daft. There didn't seem to be any girls in the team, just boys. I think they were all geeks too!'

Stonelaw didn't manage to get anything else out of Gillian Martins that was very helpful and a few minutes later he welcomed Scott Pride into the interview room.

Scott Pride was a very average looking young man with no particular distinguishing features, but the thing that was notable about him was that he seemed quite self-assured and serious, perhaps surprisingly so for such a young man.

'Mr Pride, perhaps you could tell us something about your relationship with the deceased.'

Scott Pride leant forward a little and clasped his hands together

'I can't say that I knew him all that well. We were flatmates but we had very different interests. I didn't know any of his friends really. I don't know if I can help you at all.' He leant back again and shook his head. 'It was such a dreadful, dreadful thing I've never experienced anything like this before. I don't know if I could ever go back into that house again, you know.'

Stonelaw reflected for a moment, looking him up and down.

'Miss Martins, she was your flatmate too. What was your relationship with her?'

'Oh, we weren't close but we were friends. Sometimes we'd share a curry or a glass of wine. I believe that she had become very fond of Piers. I didn't interfere. I wasn't in all that much. I spend a lot of time up in the computer lab, and I have my own friends.'

Stonelaw asked Scott Pride various other questions that all seemed to result in similar anodyne answers. Finally he said 'Mr Pride, do you play chess?'

Pride gave a little laugh. 'Absolutely not! A silly game. A basic computer program that you can download from the web can beat almost any human being. I could probably—if I put my mind to it—write a little program myself that would do it!'

About an hour later, Stonelaw was sitting over tea with his friend. He was short and plump with an almost completely bald head with little unkempt tufts of hair at the side. Rimless spectacles were perched over a short beaky nose and he sported a rather silly-looking trimmed moustache on his upper lip and, in contrast, long, rather shaggy, sideburns.

'This is Theo,' said Hamish, 'Theodore Clark. A friend from the Malt Whisky Society... and a chess enthusiast. There isn't much he doesn't know about the game.' Theo smiled, obviously pleased, and immediately began to speak in a rather rushed fashion.

'I've had a look at the position,' he said. 'It's the end of a game—white has no choice but to resign. He has probably blundered badly. It's a thematic game. White gains the bishop pair but black has a bind on the white squares. Reminiscent, I think of Smyslov-Keres, 1947. It's in *My Best Games*—not the original, the revised edition, with additional annotations. On the other hand, it could be… '

Hamish intervened. 'You also have something to tell us about the strange email.'

'Oh yes.' He took a small stapled pamphlet out of his pocket. 'This is *Scottish Chess News*, the latest edition. It's a little periodical that has been published for the past three years out of the Edinburgh Chess Club. This is volume three, number two. On pages sixteen through to eighteen there is a short article by a contributor with an unusual non-de-plume… '

'Can I see it?' Stonelaw interjected.

He examined the piece. The non-de-plume of the person in question was 'The Black Redeemer'.

Stonelaw perused the article. It consisted mostly of an annotated version of a recent game played by a retired grandmaster. The player concerned, who had been suffering from a heart complaint, had, unfortunately, collapsed and died immediately after the game. The gist of the article was contained in the last couple of paragraphs:

'In conclusion, an urban legend has been circulating for some time among chess circles especially-about a game of chess played for considerable stakes—the player's life! This legend has perhaps been popularised by the re-release of the film *The Seventh Seal* and several popular Japanese films that

154

feature deadly video tapes or DVDs, but, it transpires, there may be some substance to it after all! There are rumours that police are investigating a number of suspicious deaths of chess players throughout the country. Some say that there may be some psychopathic chess fanatic going around murdering his victims. More fanciful accounts say that it is the work of the ghost of a vengeful grandmaster or that it is a homicidal bot constructed by some mad scientist... '

'What's a bot?' asked Stonelaw.

'Oh,' said Theo, 'that's obvious. It's named after 'robot'—a chess playing machine or computer program that plays very like a real person. Bots were first popularised... '

'The Edinburgh Chess Club published this,' interrupted Hamish. 'That's the club that Campbell-Hawes had joined. The girl told us, didn't you say, Nigel?'

'That's right.' Stonelaw looked thoughtful. 'I think that maybe we need to investigate this chess society.'

'Not just a society,' said Theo, 'a place! The Edinburgh Chess Club is the second oldest chess club in the world founded in 1822, and they still have their own premises in the West End!'

Stonelaw, Hamish and Theo ascended a rather shabby winding staircase in Alva Street. Hamish had expected an ancient institution such as this to perhaps resemble the Century Club or the Malt Whisky Society—a gentleman's club with Chesterfield sofas and a polished mahogany bar— but what they found was more like a conventional tenement flat, somewhat in need of decoration. There was a hall and a little kitchen. The main room was set out with a sequence of tables with old worn chessboards as their main feature. In the corner two players were engaged in a game. Around the walls were bookshelves with well-thumbed chess books. A couple of display cabinets held the club's treasures—ancient sets of ornate chess pieces, trophies and signed letters and photographs of long-deceased grandmasters and world champions.

A tall bespectacled and affable man greeted them.

'Well, gentleman, welcome to our wee retreat from the everyday world.'

'This is Bert Burness,' said Theo, 'the club secretary.'

'Yes, indeed,' said Bert. 'Always here to accept membership applications'. Suddenly the smile disappeared from his face.

'Of course, we've had quite a tragedy. Young Piers only joined us a couple of months ago. Had a few games for the fourth team. Terrible, terrible to hear of his tragic death. We're sending a wreath to the funeral, with a little bouquet of chess pieces in the centre.'

'Mr Burness, perhaps we could talk to any of your members who knew Mr Campbell-Hawes. Also, we're interested in the *Scottish Chess News*. Would you by chance be the editor of it?'

'Oh no, not me.' He looked round the room. 'Ah! Let me introduce you to two of our keenest members,' Bert said, pointing to the two players in the corner. 'That's Vito and that's Eddie… Eddie Caldwell, he's our bidie-in and the editor of the *News*. They're in the middle of quite an exciting game. Young Vito has launched a speculative attack, but it's unlikely to fool Eddie. He's a FIDE Master, you know.'

'Yes, yes,' said Stonelaw, 'Could we talk to them please?'

'Certainly, I'll get them for you.'

'What does he mean by 'bidie-in?' Stonelaw asked Theo.

'Oh, he lives here. The Club always has a caretaker. He gets his accommodation for free and has to keep the Club open certain hours. It means he can play chess all the time.'

Vito was a pleasant young man with an Italian accent who expressed his sympathy for the sudden death of a member although, as it happened, he could not recall meeting Campbell-Hawes. Eddie Caldwell, on the other hand, did not look at all pleased at having his game interrupted. He frowned at them quite fiercely.

'Mr Caldwell, did you know the deceased, Piers Campbell-Hawes?'

Caldwell replied in a rather peremptory fashion. 'Yes, he was board six for our fourth team. Lost three, drew one. I'm having to find a replacement for him for Wednesday.'

Hamish and Stonelaw gave each other a baffled look.

'You *have* heard of the circumstances of his death?'

'Bert mentioned it, but I wasn't paying much attention. Got a tournament to prepare for in Gibraltar.'

'Mr Caldwell,' Stonelaw gave him a rather officious stare, 'it is important that you tell us anything you know about the deceased. This is a criminal investigation. A murder enquiry.'

'I know practically nothing about him. He came here asking for advice on how to improve his game. I thought it was a waste of time. He had no talent. I sent him away and referred him to Wolfgang. I didn't expect he would be much of an asset to the team, but sometimes we have a place for a board six.'

Stonelaw, with Hamish's assistance, spent another half an hour questioning the Edinburgh Chess Club members but gleaned very little from it. No-one confessed to knowing anything of any importance about Campbell-Hawes. The question of the article in *Scottish Chess News* was not resolved either. Caldwell had apparently received it anonymously in the post. He had published it, he said, because they were short of serious items that quarter.

As they left the Edinburgh Chess Club, Stonelaw suddenly thought of something. 'Hold on!' he said, 'who's Wolfgang?'

Theo smiled. 'Don't worry, it's easy enough to get hold of Wolfgang I can take you to him right now!'

Barely twenty minutes later they were ushered into an office in the King's Buildings complex of Edinburgh University. It was a very large office as there was a plethora of computers and other paraphernalia on several desks. The strains of some classical music could be heard in the background.

After a couple of minutes, a tall gentleman in a casual linen suit with slightly greying hair entered the room.

'Are you Wolfgang?' enquired Stonelaw.

'No, no,' said Theo, pushing himself forward, 'this is Dr Friedrich, the noted computer scientist.'

'Dr Freidrich,' he continued, 'I'm glad you could meet us. It has been quite some time since we met and I believe you have been very successful in several tournaments since then.' Theo indicated Stonelaw and Hamish. 'This is Inspector Stonelaw and this is my friend Hamish McDavitt. I explained broadly what we want to see you about, didn't I, on the telephone.'

Freidrich nodded to them and went over to his desk to switch off the music. 'Excuse me, gentleman. A passion of mine. But... ' he gestured toward the assembled machines on the other side of the room ' ...this is other passion This is Wolfgang.'

'Wolfgang is a computer?' asked Stonelaw.

'Not just a computer, probably the finest chess-playing computer in the world. He has taken me years to develop.

158

He is like a great composer. He creates a symphony on the chessboard.'

'I see,' said Stonelaw, 'this is the sort of program you can download from the internet that can defeat human players.'

Freidrich did not seem pleased at this description. 'Yes, But Wolfgang is much more than that. He has defeated seven grandmasters in match play including the world championship runner-up. He is coming with me to Argentina next week for a freestyle tournament. All the other major programs will be there—Fritz, Deep Blue, Shredder... '

'Dr Freidrich, we won't take up much of your time, but can I ask you a few questions?'

'Of course.'

'Did a young English student called Piers Campbell-Hawes ever come to see you about Wolfgang?'

'I don't recall the name, but I get many queries—from all over the world. Of course, he could have employed Wolfgang without seeing me. Wolfgang is commercially available.'

'You can buy it?'

'Of course. We have sold nearly half a million copies worldwide. The commercial version doesn't have the calculating power of the dual processors that come with this version, but it will beat nearly all human players running on a standard computer. Most players don't just play against him, however. They use him as a teaching aid, a coach.'

*Can you play against Wolfgang on the internet?'

'Yes.'

Stonelaw showed Freidrich the article from *Scottish Chess News*. Freidrich scanned through it. 'Is it at all possible that such a thing could exist. A death-dealing chess-playing bot?

Freidrich smiled and shook his head. 'Gentlemen, this is

159

the Computer Science department. Gothic horror is probably the preserve of English and Cultural Studies.'

Sometime later, as Stonelaw drove them back into town, they reflected on the day's events.

'Well, I must thank you for your help, Mr Clark,' he said. 'We've learnt a great deal about chess. However,' he said with an edge of frustration in his voice, 'I can't say we're any nearer solving this particular case!'

'Well,' said Theo. 'Chess is a game that goes through many stages. The Russians have a term for a particular moment. They call it 'tabiya'—the moment when the opening is over and the game has really begun!'

They all sat in the car and thought for a moment.

'Is there anything else we can do today,' asked Hamish.

'The only thing I can think of,' said Stonelaw, 'is to return to headquarters. There may be more results from forensics about the computer and the examination of the house.'

Hamish and Theo sat in the ante-room at Gayfield Square for some time, but when Stonelaw returned he seemed quite elated.

'Two things have come to light. First of all we've managed to recreate the game that Campbell Hawes played. Apparently he was playing on the internet against an opponent who had the username of the Grim Reaper'! Bit like The Black Redeemer', eh! We're trying to trace whoever it was right now.'

'And the other thing?' asked Hamish.

'Probably doesn't mean anything,' said Stonelaw, 'but when we had finished examining the room and opened the window, a little scrap of paper fell out. It was lodged in the jamb. It has some numbers and figures on it.'

'Can I see it,' asked Theo

He looked it over for a few moments. Then his eyes lit up.

'It's a simple notation of a chess position on a board. I recognize the position. It's called Philidor's legacy. It's the classical position where white sacrifices his queen to trap the king in the corner and then gives checkmate with just his knight. It was popularised by… '

'I wonder if it relates to the game in question?' asked Hamish. 'Did you get a transcript of the game, Nigel?'

Stonelaw took a paper out of his pocket. 'Here it is.'

'Do you need a chessboard, Theo?'

'No, no, don't be silly. Just give me a minute or two.'

After three or four minutes, Theo said, 'It's quite an interesting game. Can't see what it has to do with Philidor's legacy, though. It's a variation of the Blackmar-Diemar gambit in which black tries to disrupt white's queen side… '

Hamish and Stonelaw both gave a start. 'What did you say?'

'The Blackmar-Diemar Gambit.'

'The Black Redeemer!' Stonelaw and Hamish said together.

Ten minutes later they were around at Louie Delamonte's flat in Scotland Street.

'Can we just go over again what you heard in the Cumberland Bar?'

'It was all humpty-dumpty to me,' said Louie. 'I was just trying to ignore them and read my newspaper.'

'Tell me. Is this what you heard?' said Stonelaw. 'Blackmar. Diemar.' He repeated it again twice.

'Yes, that sounds very like it,' said Louie.

'That's it,' said Theo, 'it was simply a misunderstanding. There isn't any black redeemer at all.'

'Oh yes there is,' said Hamish. 'You're forgetting about the article in the *Scottish Chess News*. Somebody else had obviously thought the same thing. Do you have it there?'

Theo took the magazine from his pocket.

'Hold on, hold on,' said Louie, 'Can I see that?'

He took the magazine from Theo and looked at the back cover. 'That's the man. The man in the bar.'

'But you didn't see his face?'

'No, but I saw him pick up his pint. That's the way the cuffs of his jacket were turned up!'

They all looked at the picture on the back of the magazine. It was a photograph of the editor—Eddie Caldwell.

Hamish and Theo met at the Gayfield Square police station early the next morning for the news regarding Inspector Stonelaw's interrogation of Eddie Caldwell.

Stonelaw appeared rather bleary-eyed and ordered a rather milky and bitter coffee for himself and Theo Hamish, in anticipation of the station's choice of beverages, had brought his own tea bag, an enervating Lapsang Souchong.

'Well, we've spoken to Caldwell at length and we've let him go home.'

'What... ' said Theo

'No confession, then,' asked Hamish, 'Was he not Campbell-Hawes's companion in the Cumberland Bar?'

'Oh yes Caldwell admitted that he had been tutoring Campbell-Hawes in opening technique—he was paid, of course. And that they met in the Cumberland Bar and discussed the Blackmar-Diemar gambit. He also admits that he worked him up a bit, teasing him about his ability to play a complex opening. But he denies anything to do with the murder. He claims that he simply didn't tell us anything in fear of becoming implicated in some way. Didn't seem too concerned that withholding police evidence is a crime in itself.' I'm afraid that he's rather a selfish and thoughtless character as we thought all along.'

'And you believed this account?'

'Well, he has a watertight alibi. He was playing at a tournament in Grangemouth all night on the night in question. We've checked it out. There's no chance that he could have been anywhere near the scene of the murder.'

'What about the paper with the endgame position?'

'He agreed that it was a position he knew himself and he recognised the numbers. He showed me an example of the notation in a book. It was called the Cochrane notation or something like that. But he vehemently denied that he had written the note himself. We checked the handwriting. It's not his. Not Campbell-Hawes's either.'

'I'm not too surprised,' said Theo. 'That is, if we presume the murderer had something to do with the game on the computer. I would have reservations about Caldwell's part in that game. He's a positional player, a strategist. A free-for-all like that isn't his style at all.'

'Oh, that game,' interjected Stonewall. 'Well, there's news about that! We've found the Grim Reaper. He's a retired accountant from Leamington Spa, an amateur player of no great skill. Claims to know nothing about email messages or anything and was nonplussed at the idea of a deadly chess game. And what's more, he says that he had played Campbell-Hawes several times. He was surprised that he blundered so badly the other night, and completely shocked when he heard of his death!'

They took a moment to contemplate this news.

'Well, we're just about back where we began,' said Hamish, 'What's our next move, Theo?'

Theo thought for a short moment. 'Wasn't it Nimzowitsch who said that just about any chess player can make a forced move. When the position is stable and there isn't anything obvious to do, that's when the real master knows what the next move has to be. I believe it's in *My Finest Games*, published in… '

'Well,' Stonelaw interjected, 'What *is* our next move?'

'I haven't the faintest idea,' said Theo.

There was a contemplative silence for a moment as they all finished the last dregs of their teas and coffees.

'Let's think,' said Hamish, 'What have we learned since yesterday? This is the way I see it. Firstly, we can now discount some things. We know that Caldwell wasn't responsible for Campbell-Hawes's murder. We also know that the so-called Grim Reaper has nothing to do with it! So, maybe we could presume that the murder has nothing to do with chess at all…'

' …Which would be no bad thing,' interjected Stonelaw.

'But,' continued Hamish, 'there are still two aspects of the mystery that we cannot fully explain. Firstly, and crucially, if the Grim Reaper did not send the obituary email then who did? That is the crucial act that links the game of chess to the death. Secondly, and this looks like a bit of a long shot now, is there still any significance to the numbered scrap of paper in the Cochrane notation? We know that it's not in Campbell-Hawes's handwriting. Unfortunately, it's now possible that it could be something that he picked up at the chess club from almost anyone and have nothing to do with the case at all.'

'I don't think so,' said Theo suddenly. 'Something that has been puzzling me is why write down a position like that at all. If Campbell-Hawes was in the club someone could show it to him in a minute and he would easily remember it as it's so simple. The only reason it would be written down in that way would be if it were an example of the notation itself.' He turned to Stonelaw. 'It's the Cochrane notation. Is that what you said?'

'That's what Eddie Caldwell said.'

'No!' Theo suddenly exclaimed. That's not what he said! I think I've got it. He said Cock... rane, but he meant Cock...burn. But Eddie is English. He may be an excellent chess player, but he can't pronounce Scots. It's the Cockburn notation, pronounced Coe... burn. I remember now. I should have thought of it before! It's the notation devised by Freidrich for feeding positions into Wolfgang's database in a compact form without the aid of a visual display.'

'Dr Freidrich, the music-loving Teutonic computer genius?'

'The very same!'

They met Freidrich in his office some thirty minutes later. 'Yes, that is my handwriting.'

'And what is the type of notation and what does it signify?' asked Hamish.

'It is what I have called the Cockburn notation—named after a famous Scottish player who taught at this very University—and it signifies, in this case, a well-known chess position commonly known as Philidor's legacy.'

'Now, could you tell us why you wrote this down and do you remember when you last saw it.'

'Certainly. Of course I remember. I wrote it down as an example of the notation for a student when he was enquiring about bots.'

'A student? Piers Campbell-Hawes?'

'No, a computer science student, one of my best second years—Scott Pride.'

'Oh, that explains it then,' said Theo. 'Pride could easily have taken it back to the flat and it could have blown into the window.' He shrugged, 'Maybe it has nothing to do with the murder at all!'

'Hold on, hold on,' said Stonelaw. 'Pride told me that he wasn't interested in chess at all!'

'Murder?' asked Freidrich, 'What has Pride to do with the murder?'

'Didn't you know? He was the flatmate of the murdered student.'

'No, no-one told me that. And I spoke to Scout yesterday. He didn't mention it.'

'He didn't mention it!' Stonelaw was almost splenetic. 'He was involved in a particularly ghastly murder and he didn't mention it. Doesn't that seem strange?'

'Perhaps. Now that you come to mention it, Scott has been behaving a bit strangely. I was surprised when he asked about Wolfgang. He was mostly a systems man, not so interested in software applications. And, of course, he did so badly in his final exam!'

'But for goodness sake, he got 96%!' said Stonelaw.

'Yes, but computer science is not a subjective subject like English literature or media studies. I would expect my best students to always get one hundred percent, even if they are forty-five minutes late entering the examination room.'

'He was late! Are you sure? The exam transcript he showed me marked him down as attending for the whole time—7.00-9.00pm.

'Well, that may be so, but I was working late that night. I'm sure I saw him rush in at about 7.45pm. He was sweating and his hair was wet from the shower that had blown in.'

'Wait a minute,' Hamish intervened as Stonelaw became increasingly agitated. 'If Pride was forty-five minutes late entering the exam then technically he could have been in the flat at 7.30pm, which is within the margin of error as to the time of death. What if Campbell-Hawes had been murdered before the game against the Grim Reaper had commenced!'

'But if Pride had then left for the exam who was playing chess on the computer?' asked Stonelaw.

Hamish had been standing stock still for the last few moments, his face screwed up in intense concentration Suddenly, he became more lively.

'Theo,' Hamish enquired, 'is it possible that a bot could have been installed to play the game over the internet?'

'Oh, yes, it happens all the time. But it would be very unusual for a bot to blunder so badly as in that particular game.'

'And, Dr Friedrich, tell me, could the email messages recorded on Campbell-Hawes's computer have been send from a remote terminal?'

'Technically, they could be sent from anywhere in the world and they could be disguised to appear that they came from another terminal, or from nowhere in particular if the sender were clever enough.'

'And could they have been sent from the exam room in which Pride was ensconsed, and could Pride also have manipulated the time recorded on the exam transcript?'

'No, no, that is quite impossible,' said Freidrich. 'Student usernames have limited access to the system. Only someone with controller functions such as myself could have done that.'

'And could Pride have logged onto the system under your username?'

'Absolutely impossible! No-one knows my personal password.'

'Is that right,' said Hamish. 'Theo, do you have a pen?' Hamish took the little piece of paper and, leaning on the Wolfgang console, wrote two words on the back of it. He handed the paper to Freidrich.

'Is your password, by any chance, one of these two words?'

Freidrich's jaw dropped in astonishment. He looked at Theo, then Stonelaw, then back to Hamish again.

Scott Pride sat primly upright in the interview room at Gayfeld Square.

'When I first came to Cumberland Street', Scott Pride said, 'I was looking for a room in a flat. Campbell-Hawes was lording it over his precious interviews: 'Interviews', he called them all for the privilege of sharing a part of his stately domain. I loathed him immediately, but it was a good flat and a good room. I knew that all I had to do to get it was butter him up a bit. He was so stupid he fell for the most blunt and banal type of flattery. So he offered me the room. Then he asked where I came from and when I told him he said he needed six weeks rent as a deposit up front. I almost throttled him then. Campbell-Hawes was a poncey fool with too much money. The world isn't a fair place. I had to stack supermarket shelves every night to pay my rent and he just had to whistle and Daddy would buy him a new car. What on earth that girl saw in him God alone knows. He thought he could play chess, but he was useless at that as well. I could have beaten him by studying just for a day or so, but what was the point—a tuppence hapenny computer could do it for me. It was when he started talking about the Blackmar-Diemar gambit in that awful English accent of his that I got the idea. I started calling it the 'Black Redeemer'. It was meant to be a joke, but Campbell-Hawes was too stupid to see it. I think for a time he thought that that was what it really was called. Then I thought about it and I checked up on the internet. There wasn't a Black Redeemer on the chess web sites but after searching for a while I came across something similar—the 'Grim Reaper'. I introduced him to it, of course. Then I invented that whole phoney story about the game of life or death and sent it to *Scottish Chess News*. It was a brilliant idea and Campbell-Hawes fell for it beautifully. Such an idiot!'

'Well,' Pride paused and for the first time seemed to lose his composure just a little, but then a sardonic smile came across his face. 'You can see that he just had to die! So I killed him. I used a hammer from the toolbox in the cupboard under the stairs and an apron from the kitchen to protect my clothes. I put them in a carrier and dumped them in the old railway tunnel in Scotland Yard. I set the bot to play the game against the Grim Reaper. I devised it using Wolfgang with information I got from Dr Freidrich. The hardest bit was making sure it lost in the end. It wasn't designed to do that. It was impossible to be sure by just altering the playing level, so I had to introduce a complete blunder, an almost random move, which would be played after a certain time if the bot got too far ahead. It worked perfectly, the game finished at almost the exact time I had planned—when I was safely away from the flat. Then the bot was programmed to automatically destroy itself and I sent the email messages from the University disguising the origin and I altered the times on the exam log to provide an alibi. Of course, I needed Dr Freidrich's password. Freidrich was OK, I suppose, but he wasn't as smart as he thought he was. I'd been to his lectures and heard all that stuff about the chess game resembling a perfect piece of music. Just to make sure, I checked his birthplace from his entry in *Who's Who in Science*. It was Salzburg. Wolfgang!,' he chuckled, rocking a little forward in his chair. Wolfgang... Amadeus... Mozart. It could have been only one of two things. I was right, the password was 'Amadeus'.

'I'm not sorry I killed him. If I hadn't dropped the little piece of paper with the Cockburn notation you wouldn't have caught me. That was stupid... stupid!'

He hesitated. 'I suppose I'll go to jail.'

'I think that that is very likely indeed,' said Stonelaw.

'Can I ask you something Will I get a computer in my cell?'

That was the end of the Black Redeemer mystery for which Inspector Stonewall was thankful. Some days afterwards he could be heard muttering 'Bloody men and machines. Give me an ordinary decent crook any day.'

THE KING AND QUEEN OF SHEBA

Hamish McDavitt was walking across the Meadows after his morning constitutional up the Radical Road under the volcanic cliffs of Arthur's Seat. Today the broad grassy swathes of the Meadows was populated not only by the usual joggers and picnickers and children on their bicycles, but also by a team of fire-eaters and sword swallowers, a troupe of the ladyboys of Bangkok dressed in flamboyant saris and lush makeup, a skinny gentleman on stilts in a top hat and a group of monks seemingly organising a lynching of one of their members. All in all, it was a fairly typical day at the Edinburgh Festival, an occasion which had been memorably described by one wag as 'much like any other time in Edinburgh, but with the additional risk of being run over by a unicyclist.'

Hamish made his way down past the Speigletent in George Square Gardens, an octagonal timber-framed building in a sort of Germanic *fin de siècle* style, which advertised a theatrical production entitled 'The Flying Karamazov Brothers.' Slapped on the middle of the poster for the show was a sticker reading 'astonishing skill… *Daily Scot.*'

Then he slipped through the crowds outside a large inflated purple balloon in the shape of an upside-down cow which housed the performances at Teviot Row, walked down by The Forresthill Bar and down Candlemaker's Row with its little shops selling candles, law books, stained glass artefacts

171

and comics, and into the Grassmarket where a Festival arts and crafts fair was taking place. Among the various stalls he found what he was looking for—Lynn Landemar's knitwear stall, selling knitted jumpers, hats and scarves that she made herself in her mews house in Carlton Terrace Mews.

'Has business been good?' Hamish enquired.

'Och, Hamish. It's been really slow. I know that the summer isn't the best time to sell winter garments, but usually we get a few cold days that remind folk of the Edinburgh winter. This summer it's been just too much like… summer!'

'Well, I think I might be needing something myself,' said Hamish.

'How about a nice woolly hat with snowflakes around it to keep your head warm when you go your walks up Arthur's Seat?'

Hamish looked at the conical creation. It was long and unshapely and had two large flaps at either side. 'No. Well, not for me… not this time. I was thinking more of a nice jumper for my great-aunt Effie.'

Ten minutes later Hamish sat with a dram and a parcelled jumper in a celtic design and his copy of the day's *Daily Scot* in the White Hart Inn. This was a very old pub and it was also the very inn at which Robert Burns had lodged over two centuries ago on his visits to Edinburgh. Hamish liked it for the ambience and the Burns memorabilia on the walls. He also liked it because it was the first pub in the Grassmarket to bar stag and hen parties on drunken pub-crawls. He knew that he could read his newspaper there without a raucous invasion of Geordies or Scousers. Hamish laughed to himself at the irony of it. Stag parties banned at a pub name after a great white stag, reputedly the beast that appeared magically to King David in the 1100s in what was to become Holyrood Park.

Flicking through the reviews of Festival shows in the paper, he came across the review of the Speigeltent show that had been extracted for the poster he had seen on his walk. It actually read: 'It requires astonishing skill to eke out such an untalented and unamusing performance for over an hour.'

Hamish was chuckling at this when in walked the very author of the piece, his old friend Sean Primavera. He was dressed in shorts and trainers and carried a clipboard with a Festival Fringe programme, just what a busy reviewer about town needed on a fine summer's day.

'Ah, Sean,' Hamish said, 'I fear that your excellent work has been somewhat misinterpreted.' And he explained what he had seen on his walk earlier.

'It won't be the first or the last time,' said Sean, ordering a large Glenfiddich for both himself and Hamish. But, I'll tell you this, they won't get me on *this* one!' He explained that he had just reviewed a morning show at the Pleasance that consisted of the players mouthing nonsensical things about the nature of the universe whilst pouring stewed coffee and making gooey pancakes with maple syrup for the audience.

'It's the latest thing, cooking and performing,' he explained, 'there's a guy in a turban interviewing celebrities while cooking a curry, and a folk singer giving out Chinese carry-outs!'

'And you sampled some of the Festival breakfast?'

'Unfortunately yes. It's fair put me off my lunch,' said Sean, 'but here's what I wrote.' He handed Hamish a sheet of paper. The review began, 'The audience were divided on the merits of this production. Some thought it was the worst thing they had seen at the Festival Fringe, others thought that it was the worst thing they had ever seen.'

Hamish laughed, 'So you've had a good day so far.'

'Not so bad, actually. I only have left a new play in Scots at the Traverse and a foul-mouthed Antipodean comedian at the Udderbelly. Looks like being a lot better than yesterday.'

'What was on the agenda yesterday.'

'Ach, you wouldn't believe it. I was given a lunchtime play at the Royal Scots Club that was entirely in Portuguese! I went to the bar at the interval to try to find someone who could tell me what it was about, but there were only five people in the audience and they were all reviewers. Nobody had a clue. Anyway, we all agreed on a story we made up, so that no one would be too embarrassed the next day.'

'Not a very good start to the day, then,' said Hamish.

'And then it got worse! There was a production of *Our Town* at Adam House by some American company, the University of Hootenanny or something. Believe it or not, to fill the theatre they'd bussed in the entire population of an old folk's home! People were wandering about all through the show and some of the old biddies thought they were at the bingo and kept shouting 'house'!

'And then,' Sean continued, 'I had to hike out to a church hall for the Morningside Children's Theatre production of *Oliver*. I managed to sneak away at the interval even though they kept stuffing me with tea and digestive biscuits! Bribery isn't what it used to be. Somebody must be getting offered wads of cash or sexual favours or even a wee dram, but it certainly isn't me!'

'Is it not a little difficult to write your review if you haven't seen the whole production,' asked Hamish.

'Not at all. These things are always sold out with doting parents and relatives, so the review just has to follow a simple formula: 'Little Jimmy Smith will remarkably mature in the role of the Artful Dodger, Jenny Brown was captivating as Nancy, and once again the Wardrobe Mistress has excelled herself with her multifarious hand made creations...'

While they sat having their drams there was a little fuss outside that they hardly noticed. The unpredictable swirling Edinburgh wind had lifted the tarpaulin off a couple of the craft stalls and the whole shebang had had to be disassembled somewhat prematurely. A short while later Lynn Landemar, accompanied by a couple of the other merchants and a bucolic-looking man who ran the Well-Hung Hamburger stall, came in. They were all looking decidedly disgruntled.

'What's happened', asked Hamish.

'Robbery', said Lynn, 'barefaced robbery! We've all lost something today. I'm just missing a couple of hat-pins, but Kate here has lost some valuable jewellery.'

'And I'm missing a packet of cheese slices for the cheeseburgers!' interjected the hamburger man.

'Nobody knows how it could have happened', said Lynn, 'We were all there all day, apart from the odd short break. We've never had this sort of trouble before, and we've been here for five years.'

They sat in silence for a moment, and then Sean, who fancied himself as a bit of a sleuth said 'Now, let's think logically. This has never happened before but it has happened today. Was there anything *different* today from any other day you've been here?'

'Not at all,' said Lynn, and they all nodded.

175

Then, after a moment, a little pale-faced girl who, Hamish seemed to remember, made scented candles and pot-pourris, spoke up. 'Except for the king and queen of Sheba.'

'The king and queen of Sheba?'

'Well, yes', said Lynn, 'we've always had Long Lankin—a skinny man on stilts with a top hat who juggled clubs and balls. But he couldn't make it because he was at a fête at Prestonfield House. So this time we had the king and queen of Sheba.'

'They were very good', added Kate, 'funny, weren't they?'

'Hold on,' said Sean, 'I'm lost. Can you describe these people to me?'

'Of course', said Lynn, 'The 'queen' was a quite an ugly man with a long beaky nose. He was done up with rouged lips and mascara. He was about ten feet tall with eyelashes about a foot long. He wore a massive tiara and a long dress over his stilts. He did fire-eating and stuff—all to attract a crowd. And he had the 'king' with him, a very little fellow, maybe a dwarf. He had a black beard and wore an enormous cardboard crown and a gown with fur trimmings—when he did a handstand it fell all over him and showed off his pants. He ran about like a fool but the queen held him with a chain around his neck. They were quite an act—well worth their fee.'

'And they were around all day today?'

'Well, not quite. It was only the queen in the afternoon. The king, apparently, had had a tummy upset. But he stayed all day and was a lot of fun!'

While this conversation was taking place, Hamish was sitting quietly, examining the Kay prints on the wall—eighteenth-century caricatures of Edinburgh characters: the lanky Lord Adam Gordon, who died of his lemonade addiction, on his horse, O'Brien, the Irish giant, and little Georgy Cranstoun, who was carried around in a creel by a servant, until one day the servant put him down at the top of a hill for a rest, and when he turned round little Georgy was gone. All the citizenry of Edinburgh, of various shapes and sizes.

Hamish turned to Lynn. 'Tell me, was the queen wearing a very long dress?'

'Well, yes. It was enormous, with brocade and bobbins.'

' ...And did the queen speak to many of the stallholders today?'

'Oh' interjected Kate, 'he was *so* amusing, He told jokes and he produced chocolate eggs out of your ear!'

'And while he was amusing you all', suggested Hamish, is it possible that the diminutive king of Sheba, hidden in the voluminous robes of the queen, between guzzling slices of cheese, slipped his little hand from between the folds of the dress of the queen and snaffled items from the stalls?'

They whole company paused for a moment and looked at each other in a quizzical manner. At last Sean said 'Bravo, Hamish, it looks like you've hit the nail on the head! But,' he added, 'hadn't we better get the police on the matter right away?'

'That would be no bad thing', said Hamish, 'but I fear that the fabled queen may prove as elusive as the mythical white stag of Arthurian legend under whose sign we are now sat.'

They all sat looking rather gloomy.

'However,' he added, 'it hasn't been the best of days, so at least let me brighten up the night with a dram from the top shelf for us all. Perhaps a Tomintoul, a nutty golden evocation of waving Speyside fields of ripe barleycorn to go with the sunny Edinburgh summer evening!'

THE ST BERNARD'S SUPPORTERS CLUB

Hamish McDavitt and Nigel Stonelaw were watching football fans gathering before the local derby at the Hearts clock at Haymarket one day. A variety of wreaths from various supporters groups were scattered around the memorial to commemorate Heart of Midlothian players lost in World War One.

'Why do you think, Nigel,' asked Hamish, 'that so many Hearts players were lost in the war and so few Hibernian players?'

Nigel thought for a moment. I've really no idea.'

'It's a matter of local history. Since Hibs were a Leith team, many of the players worked at the docks in reserved occupations and didn't go to the front. The Hearts players were not so fortunate.' He paused. 'A little understanding of local history, I find, can explain so many things?'

'I don't know a lot about football myself,' said Stonelaw, 'I'm more a rugger man. Used to follow Doncaster Rovers a bit when I was a lad though.'

'Doncaster Rovers, are they a big team in England?'

'Well, sort of. Winners of the Dulux Paint Trophy in 2008. And Keepmoat Stadium holds up to fifteen thousand supporters!'

'Oh, so they have quite good attendances?'

'Not really.' Stonelaw changed the subject. 'What about you, Hamish, are you a Hibee or a Jambo as they say here?'

'Neither I'm afraid. Personally, I follow the Saints.'

'What, Saint Johnstone or Saint Mirren?'

'No, no, the Edinburgh Saints, Saint Bernard's, of course! Scottish Cup winners in 1896.'

'Never heard of them.'

'No? The first team ever to score directly from a corner. The team who beat the famous Manchester United and Arsenal in the same season?'

'Still never heard of them.'

'Well,' Hamish shrugged. 'I have to admit, they haven't actually played for a wee while. In fact, more than a hundred years. But that doesn't bother the supporters club, we still meet every couple of months in the back room of Clark's Bar. Why don't you join us… '

And so, one foggy Edinburgh night in November, in, in the back room of Clark's Bar in Dundas Street, the Annual General Meeting of the St Bernard's Supporters Club was in full swing. Apart from Hamish McDavitt and Nigel Stonelaw, there was Alan Little, the noted football statistician, known for his wry sense of humour, Calum McDonald, the mountaineering historian, and Mick Wallace, the founder of the re-established supporters club, who was chairing the meeting.

Clark's Bar was a fine traditional Scottish hostelry. There were framed photos of old customers, Swarbreck prints of old Edinburgh and old mirrors.

'Do you see than mirror over there,' asked Hamish.

'Yes,' replied Alan, "John Robertson & Son's old Scottish Whisky'. John Robertson was a famous Hearts Player!'

'But not the same one who made the whisky,' noted Calum.

'I was just thinking,' said Hamish. 'How many sons did John Robertson have?'

'Does it really matter?' asked Mick.

'I suppose not, but I was thinking about the use of the humble apostrophe. If the apostrophe was after the 's' in 'sons' then we could presume that there was more than one son.'

'What if there was no apostrophe at all?'

'Well, I suppose that would be OK. It would still suggest more than one son, but it would break the link between John Robertson and his sons and the whisky.'

'Does the inscription on the mirror therefore mean that the whisky belonged to John Robertson and his sons?'

'Yes, but if you changed it to John Robertson and his son's then it could suggest that the whisky only belonged to the son,' said Hamish.

'Or sons,' suggested Alan.

'But the possessive doesn't necessarily mean 'belonged to'. Couldn't it mean 'made by' or 'invented by?'

'I suppose so,' said Hamish.

'Anyway,' said Mick, 'we've concluded that, because of the apostrophe, John Robertson had only one son.'

'Not necessarily,' said Hamish, 'There could have been several sons who wanted nothing to do with the whisky!' He added, 'Not to mention daughters.'

Stonelaw, who had been listening in a bemused way, joined in. 'Gentlemen, is this a linguistic or a sporting gathering?'

Hamish smiled. 'Never mind, Nigel. Just honing our powers of deduction. You never know when they will come in handy! The company nodded in agreement. 'But now,' Hamish added, 'let's get on with the business'

So, they sat in the back room of the pub, with its glazed cupboard of St Bernard memorabilia and a framed photograph of the famous cup-winning team—Wilson, Robertson, Oswald, Crossan, Sneddon, Baird, Laing, McManus, Murdoch, Hall, Foyers, Paton, Clelland—adorned in their striped shirts with the St Bernard's logo, an image of St Bernard's Well on the water of Leith, and commenced the meeting.

After the voting in of office bearers (same as last year, and the year before) there was some discussion regarding changes to the club colours and badge which were considered unnecessary, a consideration of a proposal to join the Lothian District Subbuteo League which was regretfully declined, and the selection of a team for the final of the national football supporters associations sports quiz.

When the main business had been concluded and the members were relaxing with a half pint of Deuchars and a Glenfiddich, Nigel introduced a surprising new topic.

'Well, gentlemen, believe it or not, I have a real life football mystery! And a truly extraordinary case, unique in my extensive experience of solving perplexing mysteries… ' He added, ' … occasionally with a little help, of course. looking round the assembled company.

' …of one person,' he continued, 'one person seeming to be in three different places at the same time!'

'My goodness,' exclaimed Alan, with only a little hint of irony:

'I'll tell you it if, of course, you realise that it mustn't go outside this room.'

'Of course not', said Hamish. 'We're intrigued. I suggest just a short break to refresh our glasses and then we'll dedicate

181

the rest of the evening to a footballing mystery.'

'The gist of it,' began Nigel a few minutes later, 'is that Georgiou Nicklaunas, the Hibernian striker, has disappeared from his home today and it is not clear where he has got to. Normally we'd take such things with a pinch of salt, of course—footballers are known for their occasional, err… indiscretions—but the circumstances are a little unusual in this case.'

'He was playing last night, wasn't he, in the Fair Cities Cup?' enquired Calum.

'Yes, cuffed again—three nil by the Spurs!' Alan was known to be an occasional follower of Heart of Midlothian and was not, therefore, too sympathetic to Hibernian.

'Yes, Hibs were in a big European match against Tottenham Hotspur at White Hart Lane. Nicklaunas was on from the beginning but had a right shocker. Missed two sitters with his usually dependable left foot and wandered off position all night. He was injured in a high tackle from the centre half and had to be taken off after 51 minutes, but he was shortly to have been substituted anyway.'

'So, did he go missing after the match?'

'No, he came home that night. His girlfriend is heavily pregnant and expecting any minute, so he had special permission to travel to the game alone rather than with the squad.'

'And have you spoken to her?'

'Yes, earlier today. I went out to their house in Ravelston Dykes. Flash place but rather tasteless if you ask me.'

Hamish smiled, as he wasn't aware that Nigel was known for his taste and discrimination in matters of domestic style. 'She was quite distraught. Apparently, Nicklaunas had returned home that night on the last flight. He seemed disconcerted and was limping from an injury. He went to bed almost immediately and didn't even phone his mother in Armenia. She seemed to think that this was very strange as he was in the habit of phoning her every evening before bed. I asked her if she'd noticed anything else unusual about his behaviour recently 'Not especially,' she replied, but he had just had a visit from his younger brother Vasilik, who was a chef in London, and that was always difficult for him. Apparently Georgiou doted on his brother but Vasilik was impetuous and irresponsible and invariably wanted to borrow sums of money which were seldom returned.

'Anyway, we said we'd look into it and made some enquiries at the club and in various football circles. It's amazing how any news about players and such things gets around. I wasn't expecting much, but when Detective Sergeant Jeffers reported back, what he told me was quite astonishing. I just can't quite reconcile it in my head. And we're no nearer finding Nicklaunas!'

'Go ahead then,' said Mick, 'maybe we can help you solve this problem. We know a fair bit about football here, you know.'

'Well, when we collated all the reports, we found we had two reliable witnesses who claimed to have seen Nicklaunas last night, both in places where he couldn't really have been! Firstly, another young player originally from Armenia, Alexi Pavlov… '

'I know him,' said Alan, 'he's been here for a while, on trial for Hearts.'

'Yes, Pavlov had been in the Sampling Room, a large pub at Lorimer's Brewery in Gorgie, watching the game. It's mostly

183

a Hearts pub so there was a fairly neutral view of the game, most of the customers wanting neither an English team not the Hibs to win.'

Mick shook his head, smiling wryly. He knew, as an old hand in Scottish football, that there were many occasions such as this, when it seemed more important that one team, for whatever reasons of rivalry, etcetera, did not win, rather than the other team did win.

'Pavlov swears blind that he saw Nicklaunas in the pub, watching the game. He was standing in the corner, trying to be inconspicuous, and he was wearing a baseball cap and dark glasses, as if in disguise. But Pavlov insists that it was him. He even noticed that he walked with a limp when he went to the toilet near the end of the match. I asked Pavlov if he had spoken to him but he said he was so astonished to see him in a Hearts pub and obviously not wanting to be recognised, that he didn't feel he should.'

'That's quite extraordinary', said Calum, 'but there must a fair chance that it was just mistaken identity.'

'Perhaps, but the second instance is even more baffling! We also had a report from Angelico Solino, the match referee. He was returning to Italy via the international terminal at Heathrow and he saw Nicklaunas there. He was walking with a distinctive limp. However, on this occasion we had a way of checking and, sure enough, Georgiou Nicklaunas was registered on a flight to Armenia shortly after the match! We contacted his family there but his mother says she knows nothing, that Georgiou phoned last night and that she hasn't seen him. Finally, we tried to contact his brother at the hotel he works at in London, but he seems to have disappeared too, although no-one was very surprised. It appears that these jobs are a bit fly-by-night anyway, that Vasilik had gambling debts and there was a suspicion that his visa had already ran out anyway.

'So there we have it, gentlemen. At around 9.00pm yesterday evening, Georgiou Nicklaunas appears to have been a pub in Gorgie, Edinburgh, on a British Airways flight from London to Edinburgh to return home to his girlfriend, or, alternatively, boarding a flight to Armenia at London Heathrow. Can't say I can make sense of any of it!'

The company sat and thought for a little while.

'Can't seem to sort it out myself,' said Alan, 'but these eastern Europeans are temperamental types. It seems odd that he didn't phone his mother, as footballers are also very superstitious and generally stick to routine. Maybe he has hot-tailed it back to see his mother after his disappointment last night—but there again, she denies it?'

'I've an idea,' said Calum, 'it's old hat but it's the best I can do. Vasilik is Georgiou's younger brother, but he could also be his twin—twins can be born some time apart. Maybe that explains him being in two places at the one time, but not three. I don't think I've ever heard of identical triplets! And it doesn't explain why both of them would have the same limp.'

'I have no idea at all,' said Mick, 'but I do know that the famous Thomson twins both turned out for St Bernard's in the 1892-93 season. I wonder about Nicklaunas's perfect playing record this season. Maybe there are two of them and they turn our alternative games, a bit like the Proclaimers!'

The Proclaimers were two brothers from Fife who had achieved some fame in the eighties from singing self-composed anthems in a raucous manner. These were often played at football and rugby games, so this remark brought some amused chortles from the company.

'Well, Hamish, what do you think?'

'I think that you are all partly right, and, in fact, if we take all your points on board then maybe we can piece together the whole story. It seems like a proper comedy of errors, but hopefully no harm will come of it.'

'You can explain it then?'

'I think so. Firstly, I was intrigued by your notion of a person in three places at the one time. This is what the story seems to tell, but, in actual fact, note that there were only two sightings. The third location, the flight from London, is only inferred. You are assuming that from the testimony of the girlfriend. Secondly, you are quite right, Calum, that identical twins can be born some time apart. The younger Nicklaunas was perhaps a difficult birth. This would explain why he might be pampered by his mother and indulged by his brother. Also, it is not uncommon for identical twins to be like a mirror image of each other. One left-handed, the other right-handed, for example'

'I don't really see what any of that has to do with it, but go ahead anyway,' said Nigel.

'Let me put together the story as best I can. Suppose Georgiou, who has not missed a game for Hibs all season, has sustained an injury in training. That would explain the slight limp. He has not reported in but realises himself that he must miss the vital Fair Cities Cup game against Spurs. Now his brother comes to visit. Vasilik is possibly talented like his brother but also rather fickle and has always been jealous of his success. Vasilik comes up with a fantastic idea. Suppose he were to play in the match instead of Georgiou. It is a once in a lifetime opportunity. He has been an able footballer himself and it is only luck, he thinks, rather than anything else, that has ensured his brother's success rather than his. This is the moment he has been waiting for—to come good at last. He pleads with Georgiou and eventually Georgiou reluctantly, and very foolishly, agrees. Identification will be necessary to clear security at the stadium, so Georgiou and Vasilik exchange passports.

'Now the rest becomes more clear. Georgiou cannot stay at home because he has not explained the deception to his girlfriend, but he has to watch the match—not to do so would be to betray his brother and his teammates. What better place to remain incognito than in a large busy Hearts pub. So he dons a baseball cap and shades and goes to the Sampling Room. He can't foresee that the young Hearts player will recognise him. Meanwhile, Vasilik substitutes for him for the game, but, despite what Vasilik thinks of his abilities, he is no match for his brother. Also, he is right-footed rather than left-footed. This helps to explain why he plays so badly and often wanders out of position. When he is substituted he has a limp from his injury, but also his pride is hurt. He realises that really he has no talent at all. As I say, he is a very fickle young man, and spoiled. Rashly, he decides to head home to his mother and seek comfort there, and then he is seen at the airport.

'The mother, incidentally, must know the whole story by now, but she has no intention of telling the police. She will probably think that this is family business and the family will sort it out themselves.

'The rest is obvious. Nicklaunas returns home from the Changing Room, but he is distraught. He realises how foolish he has been and that he may have jeopardised his career.

Perhaps he forgets to phone his mother, or perhaps he goes to the bedroom with the telephone beside him expecting a pre-arranged call from his brother!

'But the call from his brother doesn't come. He can't sleep. He rises early and decides to catch the first flight to London to confront his brother. He will be back as soon as possible so there is no need to tell anybody… '

'So he is in London, then?'

'I'm afraid not. Remember, he had Vasilik's passport and Vasilik's visa had run out. The immigration authorities would not have let him alight at Heathrow. They would have insisted he return to Armenia. I expect he is sitting there now, shame-faced, after trying to explain the whole situation to his mother.'

The whole company looked amazed as they took a moment to take in the complexities of Hamish's explanation. At last Nigel said, 'My goodness, If you're right, Hamish, what should we do now?'

'I would simply reassure his young lady that he will be back soon, but not too soon. Georgiou will probably need a little time to consider what to tell his manager, Herr Vogts, which, considering his reputation for having a very prickly temper indeed, will not be very easy!'

SPELLING LESSONS

Hamish McDavitt and Nigel Stonelaw were sitting in the unusual but reasonably pleasant surroundings of the Elephant House on George IV Bridge drinking, respectively, a jasmine tea and a cappuccino. Across from them, at a bench adjacent to a display of crayon drawings of various shapes and sizes of pachyderms, sat Charlie and Laura, the Stonelaw grandchildren, scoffing frothy hot chocolate and chocolate muffins.

Detective Inspector Stonelaw was generally bemoaning the lot of the unwilling child minder. 'We've been to the top of the Scott Monument and the Castle. I can't think of what else. And to top it all, we're missing the Scotland v Ireland match at Murrayfield.' He looked a little forlorn.

Hamish knew that Nigel Stonelaw was a great rugby man and also, unfortunately, somewhat lacking the skills required to entertain young children.

'Ah, well', Stonelaw shrugged. 'Children. I suppose they're not something you've had to think about yourself, Hamish, being an old bachelor.'

'Not so old!' Hamish replied, 'and also not always a bachelor.'

Stonelaw seemed surprised. 'You never mentioned that you were married, Hamish.'

'Some time ago, and only for one year.'

'Oh. Didn't work out then?'

'No,' Hamish replied, 'it didn't work out. She died.'

'Oh!'

'Well,' Hamish interjected before Stonelaw could think how to extricate himself from an awkward silence, 'I tell you what. Why don't you go down to Deacon Brodie's and catch the rest of the rugby. I'll entertain the children for a little while.'

A few moments later, Hamish was sitting with the children inspecting their artistic efforts. 'Well, did you like going to the Castle and all that?'

'No,' said Charlie, the smaller and the younger of the two, 'it's boring!'

'Ah', said Hamish, 'so what *do* you like, then?'

Laura answered, 'Grandma took us to see *Henry Porter and the Crucible of Blood*. It was great. Bad men were going to burn all the nice witches and Henry Porter had to save them.'

Hamish thought for a moment. 'Well, do you know that we used to have lots of witches and wizards in Edinburgh too, and just around the corner from here. And do you know too, that the nice lady who wrote all the stories about Henry Porter used to come here and drink hot chocolate just like you.'

'Gosh!' said Charlie, 'did she... and did they burn witches at the stake and all that, just like roast beef?'

'That's a different kind of steak,' said Laura.

'Yes, indeed,' said Hamish, 'we burned lots and lots of witches here in Scotland. We were very keen on it. The King himself had a hand in it. Let's see, there was the two-faced Major Weir and... '

'Can we go and see where the witches were?' said Laura.

So Hamish took them down Victoria Street and showed them the little shop with all the brushes and brooms and domestic items made of wood in the window

'This is where the witches used to buy their broomsticks and wands and everything like that, and across the road, where that pub, the Bow Bar, is now, there was a pub called the Cauldron, where they all used to meet.'

'Gosh!' said Charlie.

'Let's go across', said Hamish. Next to the pub was a shop advertising walking tours of haunted Edinburgh. 'We'll go in and get a programme,' said Hamish, 'and maybe your Grandad will let us go on a tour later.'

He took them back across the road to the joke and novelty shop where they bought some Halloween masks and a luminous inflatable skeleton. Then down the Grassmarket past the Last Drop and Maggie Dickson's pub where he told them about 'hauf-hangit' Maggie who had been hanged at the gibbet but was discovered alive when she banged on the lid of her coffin. Then up the Castle Steps to the Witchery and the Camera Obscura. By now Charlie was getting a little tired and they sat at a bench the public concourse to the Castle and had some ice cream that Hamish had bought.

'Do you know any stories about wizards and witches?' asked Laura.

'Oh, lots,' said Hamish, rather optimistically as he was not altogether sure that he did.

'Go on and tell us one then,' said Laura.

'Please... ' said Charlie.

'Well... ' Hamish said, thinking of the last time he had been to the Scottish Storytelling Centre at John Knox's

House and of how adept some of the participants had been at improvising stories from a standard formula. After thinking for a few moments he started. 'Well, one time many years ago, there was a terrible stooshie amongst all the witches and wizards in Edinburgh.'

'What's a stooshie?' asked Charlie.

'It's an awful fuss,' said Laura, 'Grandma told me. Like when Grandad found all the potatoes in the hall cupboard.'

'However,' Hamish, who was quite familiar with the story of the lost tatties, continued, 'this particular stooshie was caused by a naughty little witch who had bright green hair and a little button nose that she used to cast spells and her name was Suzy Scott.'

'Was she related to Walter Scott. They called him the wizard' asked Laura.

'Well yes, You're right,' said Hamish. 'He was the wizard of the north. But she was related to *Michael* Scott, another Scott. He was a real wizard!'

Hamish continued. 'Suzy was being very naughty indeed and was going around leaving tickling spells all over the place. Now a tickling spell is a terrible thing because when you find one, it's like being tickled all over by lots of hands and you can't stop laughing for half an hour.'

Charlie found this so funny that he started tickling Laura all over and only stopped when she tweaked him hard on the nose.

'There were tickling spells all over the place, hidden in the folds of bedclothes, and in bottles of milk, and in the pages of books and newspapers like the *Warlock Times*. Now, all the wizards and witches were getting very sick of this because they couldn't get any work done and the Spellfinder General had to spend all his time smelling for the tickling spells until his nose turned all creamy, like a kind of cheese, and began dripping all over the place.'

Charlie and Laura thought that this was very funny and felt their own noses to see if they were falling off.

' …And they had looked everywhere for Suzy Scott. But Suzy couldn't be found anywhere at all, because she was hiding.' Now, Hamish paused, 'how do you think that she could hide herself in Edinburgh all those years ago when it was much smaller than today?'

'She could have turned herself into a dormouse, or a toad, like in Henry Porter,' said Laura.

'Maybe she found a very dark or a very small place, like under the bed or behind the curtains. That's how we hide,' said Charlie.

'Perhaps,' said Hamish, 'but remember she had to get about the town to plant her tickling spells? How do think she could hide but still move around among all those people?'

The children thought very hard and screwed up their faces just as Hamish sometimes did when he had to solve a mystery.

'I know,' said Laura after a little while, 'sometimes when we play tig I hide there's loads of other people, like when everyone's coming out of the gym at school.'

'Very good,' Laura,' replied Hamish, 'Have you ever heard anyone say that the best place to hide a tree is in a forest?'

By this time they had started walking back down the hill and were coming up to the High Street and lots of fans were walking down on their way back from the rugby. And, as it seemed, there were lots and lots of Suzy Scotts around, for the Irish fans were wearing bright green wigs!'

'There she is, and there, and there… ' said Charlie.

193

Hamish smiled. 'Yes that's it exactly. As it happened, when Suzy Scott was planting her tickling spells, there were lots of Irish wizards and witches and leprechauns in Edinburgh for the broomstick Olympics, and that's why the Spellfinder General couldn't find her!

'Anyway, when all the Irish leprechauns had gone back home, the Spellfinder General took just two shakes of a dragon's tale to find Susy Scott and took her to the Court for the Misuse of Mischievous Magic. First they thought they would tie her thumbs and her big toes together and throw her into Dunsappie Loch, near Arthur's Seat, to see if she could swim, but then they decided that it was best that she should be punished by a spell that made all her hair fall out, and her nose grow six inches and her mouth turn downwards as if she were always frowning.'

'She must have looked a bit like Grandad, then,' said Laura.

'Oh I don't know about that,' said Hamish, suppressing a smile. 'But I do know that you'll always have a very pretty face and, when you're grown up, you may become a very good detective yourself?'

THE WORLD TURNED UPSIDE DOWN

Hamish McDavitt, sometimes known as the 'wee dram detective' because of this propensity for solving mysteries with the aid of a dram of whisky, was having a leisurely lunch in the Malt Whisky Society in St Giles Street with a few friends and having that very thing—a wee dram. They were testing barrel 295, a mature Scapa, with its characteristic tones of heather and lavender and its distant notes of sea breezes and barnacled boat bottoms.

Alex Coulthard, the antiquarian book dealer, was relaxing in one of the traditional leather, button-backed winged lounge chairs and glancing through the *Daily Scot* when suddenly he sat up with a start.

'Well, that's a strange thing!'

Hamish had been quite absorbed by an article about baby-farming in Stockbridge in the current journal of the Cockburn Society that had been written by his friend Superintendent Robert Ord, but the exclamation was so forcibly ejected that he sat up in his chair. 'What's that you've found?' he asked, realising that Alex was pointing in an animated fashion to a piece in the paper.

It turned out that the gist of the short piece that he was indicating was that an old age pensioner, James McIsaac, of Duke Street, Leith, had been mugged in Salamander Street late the previous evening and had died in hospital. Police were asking for witnesses who might have seen the old man, wearing an aged grey mackintosh and a trilby hat, in the vicinity that evening.

'I'm pretty sure it's the same man,' said Alex. 'Not many people dress like that now! He came into the shop yesterday afternoon with three books wrapped in old brown paper. They were clearly old and of some value but I wasn't able to make him a serious offer without some research. However, he didn't seem to want to take them away with him. He said he would take two hundred pounds for the three. I agreed, I was pretty sure that was a fair figure. One of the books is extremely unusual. Maybe just up your street.'

So, an hour or so later they were in Coulthard's bookshop in the basement of the terrace at the top of Leith Walk. This was one of Hamish's favourite places in Edinburgh, a treasure trove of old books, pamphlets, maps and ephemera through which one could browse for hours. The shop itself hadn't changed for decades although Alex Coulthard had only bought it over some five years previously after the death of the previous owner. Alex was not exactly a bibliophile or even a particularly astute dealer in this business, but he had inherited some money from his maternal grandmother and he found the bookshop an amenable diversion compared to the tax office in which he had once worked. One thing that he had not tried to change was the endless stream of female shop assistants that had been employed in the shop over the years. They were of all ages but all had the same plummy accents and generally wore old-fashioned knitted jumpers. Edinburgh seemed to reproduce these people generation after generation. They were invaluable to Alex as they seemed quite at home in sometimes gloomy environment of the shop and didn't demand to be paid very much. Alex had no idea what they did with the rest of their lives and thought it impudent to ask.

The shop was arranged as a series of interconnected rooms. The most valuable of the stock was kept in the most central of the rooms, where there was a desk, a series of glazed bookcases and a small safe for the most valuable items. This is where Coulthard found the volume in question.

The book was in an old but undistinguished binding—which Alex suggested was possibly from around 1900—with a dirty and tattered paper dust jacket. The contents of the book itself were obviously much older.

'Probably early eighteenth century, I would guess, although there's no date. It came with another two volumes, bound collections of old chapbooks—not tremendously uncommon, but very collectable.'

The book itself was indeed unusual. No imprint or date, or even a named author or title. Just page after page of dense text in what looked like Latin with little or no punctuation. Apart from this, the most interesting feature of the book was four prints—copper engravings. They were extremely detailed, with many different scenes packed into each as seemed possible. They were not dissimilar to the fantastic paintings of Hieronymous Bosch. There were little scenes of people and animals copulating men with thistles for heads, haggises running around on three legs, couples fighting with forks and spoons for weapons. In all, a crazed vision of a strange, perverted world.

'Very strange indeed,' offered Hamish, 'And no obvious clue as to what it is all about.'

'No, and unfortunately I can't make head or tail of the text. It could be a form of Latin. Do you know any Latin, Hamish? I'm ashamed to say I don't myself. My school was progressive enough to insist that we all learned French.'

'Only a little, I'm afraid. But God alone knows what this is!' He scanned it for a while and flipped through the page. 'Look, there's a sort of foreword at the beginning. At least that might give us a clue.'

They both spent about ten minutes perusing what looked like two hundred words of gobbledegook.

At last, Hamish looked up from the book. 'I think I have something. The words are in Latin as you suggested, but they are written backwards! Unfortunately, my Latin is only schoolboy stuff, but I think I can make out a few words.'

He took out a notebook and copied some words: 'rebil, sidnum, musrus, musroed.' Then he wrote them out again in reverse: 'liber, mundis, sursum, deorsum.'

'It seems to say 'the book of the world turned upside down'!'

Alex was quite impressed by this and gave out a soft whistle. 'The book of the world... turned upside down! It sounds familiar, but what does it mean?'

'Well, actually, I do know something about this. The concept of the world turned upside down is old. It goes back to medieval times, I believe. In Umberto Eco's great medievalist novel, he refers to the upside down world as something found originally pictured in the margins of a psalter. He calls it 'a topsy-turvy universe, in which dogs flee before the hare, and deer hunt the lion'. In more recent times, the expression has been used to refer to revolutions and to labour riots. There are quite a few pubs in England by that name, one features in a novel by Peter Ackroyd that is about the supernatural and devil worship!' Hamish paused for a breath. 'But that's all I know. There's probably a lot more that we can find out at the library.'

'So we don't really know what it's all about yet?'

Hamish looked puzzled. 'I just don't know, but I may be able to work out the meaning of this page at least. I'll transcribe it, then maybe we can both do some research.'

Hamish was heading back up towards his home on Royal Terrace when he turned the corner and, literally, bumped into an old acquaintance. Giovanni Solari, also known as the Great Solari, was a stage magician of the old school, specialising in showmanship and grand illusions. Hamish had come to know him through his research into conjuring and prestidigitation that had been a help in some of the cases he had been involved with.

Solari's face creased into recognition.

'Ah, Hamish, old friend. Do you remember me, the Great Solari, magician and illusionist.' He made a pretence of dusting down Hamish's jacket. 'My apologies. I was so taken up with a new illusion I'm planning that I wasn't looking where I was going!'

Hamish resisted the urge to feel for his wallet. He couldn't remember Solari ever doing anything by accident.

'Of course I remember you, Giovanni. How are you? It's been some time.'

'Yes, I suppose it has—but I'm still up to the old mischief, plunging the depths of diablerie and magick! How about yourself, still solving mysteries?'

It suddenly occurred to Hamish that Solari was also known

as something of an expert on the occult and had a collection of books of that nature. 'I'm just working on a little mystery, in fact, that may be of interest to you. Would you like to have a look at a very unusual book?'

Solari asked Hamish to describe the book and Hamish gave him some details of the general dimensions and contents.

So, a couple of hours later, Hamish was back at Coulthard's bookshop. Solari had shown a great deal of interest in the volume and had promised to look in on his return from planning a new show at the Queen's Hall.

Coulthard seemed quite agitated. 'There's something else, Hamish, that I've just discovered. There's some scraping around the lock on the front door and I've checked the back window. It's barred, of course. But there are fresh footprints and finger marks. It's possible that someone was around here last night, checked to see if they could get in. But it's not easy around here. The front is too public and I have a fairly new alarm system.'

'Hmm… ' Hamish thought, 'It could be nothing, but perhaps someone wants the enchanted book and doesn't want to pay your prices.'

Alex shrugged. 'Well, let's just hope your magical friend has some answers. I'm not sure I entered the antiquarian book business to be involved in mysteries like this. I prefer detective novels! I'm getting jittery about the whole thing.'

A few minutes later, Solari came in. Alex, who knew nothing much about magicians apart from what he had seen in old films, thought that he looked exactly as he had expected. A mop of half greying hair flopped around his forehead. He had precisely trimmed and pointed sideburns and an elfin beard. A macaroni type of cravat was fixed around his neck and he wore a brightly coloured satin jacket. His mannerisms were extravagant and he had the air of someone who liked to command an audience.

'Ah, this must be your antiquarian friend,' he said, acknowledging Alex with a nod of the head, 'and this, perhaps, is the book in question.'

It was indeed, the book in question that he had spied and he sat down at the desk to examine it. From his jacket, he took another book of a similar size and opened it to show pages of strange-looking symbols. He sat it beside *The World Turned Upside Down* and asked for a magnifying glass to compare the two. After a while, he asked if there was such a thing in the shop as an Aramaic dictionary and Hamish and Alex, after a couple of minutes searching the shelves, found one for him.

Solari fiddled for a while with the dictionary, moving to and fro and looking to the heavens with a furrowed brow before he handed the dictionary back to Coulthard. 'I don't think I need it after all,' he said, leaning over the book and again examining it closely with the magnifying glass. He took one last long look and then shut it firmly.

'Gentlemen, have you ever heard of the Devil's Bible?'

'Yes,' said Hamish, 'there's a story by a well-known Orkney writer about it. It is a book that is cursed and brings disaster to whoever possesses it.'

'Well, I can tell you that this book is just as dangerous. In fact, I have a suspicion about it. Have you heard of Major Weir?'

Hamish and Coulthard nodded. They were both familiar with the story of Major Thomas Weir, an Edinburgh preacher of the seventeenth century who had confessed to incest and consorting with demons. He had been strangled and burnt

201

at the stake, but for centuries afterwards strange visions and happenings had been reported around his house in the West Bow.

'Well, it is sometimes said that Weir was in possession of a book very like this. It is also said that he sent it to Symson's Printing House in the Trongate, under oath of secrecy, to be copied—just before Symson's house burnt down. If you wish to check this I believe there is a mention of ane buke of a de'il' in Sinclair's *Satan's Invisible World Uncovered*. You may well have a copy?'

'Yes I have,' said Coulthard, 'but only the Tuckwell Press reprint. The original is quite rare.'

'It says here, I believe,' Solari continued, picking up the book and holding it in the air close to his face, running a long finger with his distinctive filed, pointed and polished nails across a page and reading in a rather a hushed but still melodramatic voice rising to a slight but distinctive crescendo, 'He who can read Satan's code without aid will become his lieutenant in the underworld. He who translates it is ill advised and will burn in hell's fires!'

Solari closed the book and gave them both a piercing look.

'Gentlemen, I advise you to take caution. You cannot sell this book. If you do so you will be doomed. Remember the fate of poor McIsaac.'

'You've heard of McIsaac's death then,' asked Alex.

Solari frowned slightly, as if he had been caught 'Oh yes, of course, I read about him in the paper, and his initials, you'll have noticed, are written in pencil on the title page of the book. I knew him. He was a magician himself at one time, a very powerful one. It was rumoured that he had kept a book such as this for many years. As you know, he had deteriorated recently. When I heard of his death I wondered what had happened to the book. Now I know.'

Hamish was about to ask Solari a question but Coulthard, now seeming rather agitated, butted in: 'What do you mean that I can't sell the book.'

'Tradition has it that the book cannot be traded for earthly money. Death will visit he who tries to do so. You can only dispose of it by giving it to someone who will accept it in full knowledge and of his own free will. Such a person may be hard to find. Perhaps, however, you will be fortunate. There is also a legend, I believe, that the book may suddenly disappear spontaneously and return in another place at another time.'

He took the book and placed it in the safe that was lying open. 'I cannot advise you what to do, but keep it secure for the time being. The book has powers that are not to be tampered with.'

He turned to leave, then turned back, opening his jacket and feeling his inside pockets.

'Excuse my caution, gentlemen, but I must be sure that I do not leave with anything that belongs to that book, or else the curse may pass on to me.' He nodded and left with a flourish as if completing one of his stage tricks.

Alex seemed quite disturbed. 'I don't think I like this, Hamish. I don't like this at all! I've never had the Devil in my shop before.' He looked disconsolate. 'And I don't think the customers will like it either,' he added, 'That stuff's for the little witchery shop up in Candlemaker Row.'

Hamish smiled a little. 'Well, let's take Solari's comments with a pinch of salt for the time being. He *is* a master of melodrama?' He looked thoughtful for a moment. 'It is, however, rather perplexing that he knew all about McIsaac!'

Even though his death was in the papers, it's peculiar that Solari should just happen to know something more about the book.' Hamish paused to reflect, then he shrugged. 'Anyway, shut up the safe and the shop. We'll do our research and see what we come up with tomorrow.'

Alex Coulthard rose early the next morning and strode purposefully from his deco-style apartment on Orchard Brae up to Hamish's house on Calton Hill. Coulthard had been raised in a rather chaotic house in the Grange—his father a brilliant if erratic mathematics lecturer at the University and his mother a continual enthusiast for various fads and causes. In opposition to his upbringing, he had, after attaining a suitably average degree, got an office job in an insurance company and married an averagely attractive clerical worker from the same firm. Perhaps unsurprisingly, he had soon discovered that neither his employers nor his ambitious young wife really cared for his rather detached dreamy manner and he found himself alone and without any notable purpose in life. He had been rescued from this impasse when his parents had offered him a sum of money to buy over the secondhand book business which was now his own. He had discovered a real aptitude for this business—he liked reading and books—especially detective stories (which was partly the reason he was acquainted with Hamish McDavitt)—but had no real desire to acquire or possess them, leaving that to his customers.

When he arrived Hamish was brewing a breakfast cup of Darjeeling. He offered Coulthard a cup.

'Have you deciphered the text yet?' Coulthard asked, an enthusiastic edge to his voice.

'Just a little of it, as best I can.' Hamish took a little notebook from his desktop. 'This is what it says.' He read slowly and carefully from his notes.

'This is the book of the world turned upside down inscribed and pictured by Juan Antonio de Pulgar who rests at Satan's right hand. Beware all who read it lest you too be damned.'

'That's it,' said Hamish. 'Quite explicit.'

'I take it that you haven't deciphered the rest yet then, Hamish, as you haven't been spirited off or met the untimely fate of the late McIsaac!'

Hamish looked a little puzzled. 'You seem to be treating the whole thing rather casually this morning, Alex, considering how concerned you seemed to be yesterday.'

'Ah, well, yes, sorry, Hamish. I suppose I should have told about this right away. I found it in an old edition of the *Antiquarian Book Collector*, it's an article by the noted bibliophile Gershon Cunningham.' He handed Hamish a volume marked at one page by a Coulthard & Co bookmark. Hamish read the piece.

'Juan Antonio de Pulgar was a seventeenth-century Spanish nobleman who confessed on the rack to having visions sent by the Devil. He begged for mercy and, in response to his request, the Inquisition judged that he should be burnt at the stake subsequent to having his legs and arms removed and all his orifices filled with boiling oil. Tradition has it that his visions were transcribed into code and printed in a magical book called *The World Turned Upside Down* in around 1665.

No such book has been proved to exist although something similar is listed in the proceedings of the Parisian group the Cercle du Livre Précieux, who specialised in erotic literature in the fin de siécle. If such a work were to be found, its value would be inestimable. However, it is likely that the story is apocryphal. What we do know, beyond doubt, is that a sort of spoof of this work, comprised mostly of nonsense in dog Latin printed in reverse was produced in around 1795 and circulated around members of the Hellfire Club in London and the Knights of the Cape in Edinburgh. Its purpose was simply as a curiosity and to fuel the contemporary interest in all things salacious and Satanic. The most interesting aspect of the book is the four engravings, purported to be of an earlier date and, allegedly, the work of the noted print and map maker, Richard Blome. These volumes are by no means as scarce as some booksellers may pretend, and, while an interesting curiosity, are not particularly valuable, fetching £200-300 at auction.'

'So there's nothing magical at all. Just a lot of palaver over nothing.'

'Maybe so,' said Hamish, screwing up his face as he was sometimes prone to do when he was struggling to understand something. 'But James McIsaac is still undoubtedly dead and, if there were nothing to it why did Giovanni Solari make such a show of examining it?' He rose to his feet in a determined fashion. 'Let's go. I think it may be time to have another look at the thing!'

When, twenty minutes later, however, Coulthard took the book from the safe, he almost dropped the volume in shock.

'My God, Hamish. There's nothing in it. The pages are blank. Solari was right. It has disappeared into another time, another place!'

'Hmm, perhaps,' said Hamish, examining the volume carefully. Then he shut it with a thud and turned to Coulthard in a determined fashion. 'However, I know a little more about Jimmy Smith, aka the great Solari, than you do. He's a trickster, a very clever one, but a trickster all the same. I can't really believe that there's anything magical here.'

He took the book from Alex. 'Would you mind putting the kettle on. I think the occasion calls for a cup of tea.'

They sat down and had their tea, but before it was poured, Hamish passed the open pages of the book over the steaming spout of the kettle and, amazingly, a series of symbols and characters appeared on the pages.

'The old schoolboy trick. Invisible ink. When Solari made such a play about not leaving with the book on his person, we forgot that he was also leaving without the volume, the dictionary of symbols, he brought in. This is it. The cold of the safe has made the text disappear. When he had us searching for an Aramaic dictionary he switched the dust jackets on the two. When we returned he was bent over the book seemingly examining it with the magnifying glass, but he was really hiding it from us. Then he closed it and put it in the safe.'

'But where is the *World Turned Upside Down* then? He made such a point of showing us that he wasn't taking anything away with him.'

'Not far away, I expect,' said Hamish, 'Where better to hide a book but in a bookshop?' And he was correct, for after a few minutes search, they found it, nestling between a selection of bound volumes of the *Proceedings of the Society of Antiquaries of Scotland*.

'I don't understand,' said Coulthard. 'If he didn't want the book then why did he go to the trouble of hiding it in the first place, and why all that nonsense about damnation and disappearing and all that.'

'I'm not quite sure. But one thing I know about magicians,

they are very good at providing what we call in the detective business red herrings. Distracting you while they do something quite different under your nose. Let's have another cup of tea and think about it.'

They sat in silence for a few minutes. 'Excellent tea' Hamish said. 'Lady Grey perhaps??

Coulthard checked the packet. 'Right again, Hamish,' He was becoming rather peevish. 'But do you have a solution to the book mystery?'

'I have a little idea. Suppose this was nothing to do with the *World Turned Upside Down* book at all! Do you have the other books you got from McIsaac, the chapbooks?'

'Yes, in fact they've been lying on the desk here all the time. With all the palaver I completely forgot about them.'

Coulthard provided the books and Hamish leaved through them. They were in a rudimentary binding and consisted of chapbooks from around the period 1790-1820 adorned with amateurish woodcuts and with titles like *An Astonishment: Man With Three Legs and Four Thumbs*; *The Learned Pig. Who Can Spell And Count*, *Magician With Cloven Hoof Sighted In Kirkcaldy And Raises Cain*.

Soon he found what they were looking for. 'There's something missing here.' said Hamish. 'Look, a few pages have been cut with a razor blade and removed. I'm willing to bet that this is Solari's work.'

'What can it be that he wanted. Just an old chapbook or broadside?'

Hamish shrugged. 'I think, in the circumstances, the only thing we can do is ask him.'

Solari ushered them in to his drawing room. Books and trunks were dotted around the floor. On one wall was a large painting of a figure with the bottom half of a goat and the hirsute upper body of a man with twisted horns growing from his head.

'Don't be alarmed, gentlemen,' said Solari. 'It is merely a satyr, a servant of Dionysus. Not the Devil. If you wish to see the Devil, I suggest you look in the window of one of the townhouses in Gayfield Square, halfway up, heading east.'

They sat down at the table and Hamish brought out the books, four separate volumes.

'Here we are, Jimmy,' said Hamish. Solari winced at the use of his original name. 'No time for any more tricks. We know how you substituted the books. All we need to know is what you took from the bookshop and why. And you had better tell us the truth. Remember a man has died in this little affair.'

Solari reflected for a moment then nodded slowly. 'OK, the game is up, as they say in those silly detective stories you like so much. I'll tell you everything.

'Firstly, let me assure you that McIsaac's death had nothing to do with you or I or the books in question. He was a very foolish old man and up to his neck in it with prostitution and gambling, I expect that that is why he needed the two hundred pounds you gave him. Any one of the unsavoury characters he mixed with could have done for him, or it could have been just a random mugging. His health was very poor and he was becoming increasingly frail, partly because of his debauched way of life.

'No matter how foolish he was, however, he had been a magician himself and he had been initiated into the Magic Circle of Kronos. In fact, he also initiated me, many years ago. Only members of the Circle can possess the *Handbook of the Circle*—it contains the secret litany. Each volume is individually printed when a new member is inducted. That is why, when I heard of McIsaac's premature death, I went down to his smelly little flat in Duke Street to find his copy, before it could pass into the hands of unbelievers. When I found the receipt from Coulthard & Co I knew what must have happened. I did investigate the possibility of raiding the shop in the early hours of the morning, but your security was too tight and, besides, I knew I could trick my way into getting the *Handbook*. I was on my way to the shop when I saw you, Hamish, leaving. I suspected you would have something to do with it so I contrived to bump into you. You told me about the supposedly magic book, so I was prepared for that, but I also knew that McIsaac collected old broadsheets with a magical inclination. So when I came to the shop I guessed where I might find what I was looking for. The rest you know.'

'But why did you just not ask me for the book, or buy it?'

'You might not have agreed. Imagine if such a thing were put up for auction. The Circle would be disgraced! Besides, unbelievers shouldn't be allowed to view the secrets of the Circle.'

He rose from his chair. 'Anyway, there is nothing you can do now. The *Handbook* is safe in the hands of the Circle again. Arrest me!' He made a melodramatic gesture and raised his hands together to chest level. Suddenly a pair of handcuffs appeared as if from nowhere, binding his wrists.

'Do not be surprised,' he said, snapping his arms apart making the handcuffs suddenly disappear. 'Prison holds no fears for the Great Solari. Chains or prison cells cannot hold me. So take me to the police station… ' He paused. It is just around the corner.'

He sat down, 'Alternatively, however, you might let me just pay for the books?'

'You certainly can', said Alex. 'Two hundred pounds, please. Exactly what I paid your late friend. And you can keep the upside down book too—I'll be glad to see the back of it! I think I'll stick to modern first editions in the future.'

Solari took a cheque book from his pocket and signed a cheque with a flourish. 'Here we are. Make sure that doesn't disappear!'

Alex looked at him suspiciously.

'I'm only joking, of course. Look, it's an ordinary ball point pen. Here, take it away with you if you wish.'

It was only a few minutes later when they were crossing Gayfield Square smelling the hawthorns and rowans in bloom mingling with the not so pleasant fumes of stale body odour and Carlsberg Special from the down-and-outs on the park benches, that Coulthard stopped dead in his tracks.

'Good God, Hamish, what if it was the original lost volume of Juan Antonio de Pulgar after all, or the copy procured by the diabolical Major Weir! It would be worth a small fortune.'

'Well,' said Hamish, 'I think it highly unlikely that such a thing ever existed. However, I did examine it a little more thoroughly. You may have noticed some figures in the margin of the book: CVCCDM.'

'Roman numerals!'

'Indeed, and since it was an upside down book I turned it upside down: MDCCVC—1795.'

'So it was just a cheap copy after all!'

'Perhaps, but if you had examined it a little further you

might have found a little local interest. It was signed, on the front page, 'Sir Lluyd'.'

'Not Major Weir then. Doesn't mean anything to me.'

'In fact, Sir Lluyd was the appellation of one of the Knights of the Cape, someone known quite well in Edinburgh. His name was Deacon Brodie, who met an unfortunate end, though not from reading any mumbo-jumbo.'

Coulthard was all too aware of the story of the infamous Deacon, supposedly a model for Stevenson's Dr Jekyll and Mr Hyde, a respectable cabinetmaker by day and a rogue and a thief by night. 'Oh no! So it probably is worth something after all!'

'Yes, and we'll be able to find out,' said Hamish, taking the book from the inside pocket of his jacket. Jimmy Smith isn't the only conjuror around. I switched it for the book of symbols the same way he had in the shop, while he was signing the cheque.'

Coulthard scratched his head and laughed in amazement at his friend's ingenuity. 'Hamish, you're a wonder!' He thought for a moment. 'But we can't take this, can we. After all, Solari has paid for it with good money. It would be theft!'

'If indeed he has paid for it,' said Hamish, 'let's just have a look at the cheque in your inside pocket.'

And when Coulthard took the cheque from his pocket he got another shock, for the signature was there alright, clearly scratched along the bottom right hand corner. But there was nothing else on the paper! Everything, including the bank details had disappeared.

'Smoke and mirrors For Solari, everything is show and artifice! I do tend to enjoy our occasional encounters.'

'So all is well then?'

'Yes indeed. Now I know that it is very rude to look in people's windows, but if we cross the road just here it might be our only chance to get a glimpse of Satan.'

'What's all that about, Hamish?'

'Another of my cases, and one that wasn't quite so easy to solve! But we'll keep that for another day.'

THE FIRST AND LAST MYSTERY

It was a fairly balmy day, for Edinburgh, in the early summer. Hamish McDavitt had returned to his flat in Royal Terrace after dining at Lynn Landemar's little mews house in Carlton Terrace Lane. Two years previously, when Hamish had had to have an operation on his foot and was partially immobile, he had employed Lynn, a divorced mother of two teenage girls, to help with his household chores. Once he recovered, he fully intended to fend for himself—as he had for many years since the premature death of his wife.

However, Lynn would not hear of it, firmly insisting that a single man of slightly advanced years was not at all capable of looking after himself. So, most days, Lynn was round at 30 Royal Terrace, top flat, washing dishes, preparing nutritious meals and laying out socks neatly, in pairs. Recently, also, she had insisted on inviting him round for dinner once a week.

These occasions were pleasant, with mostly experimental pasta dishes and homemade elderberry wine. Lynn's two daughters, Belinda and Jade, would flit in and out, whispering to each other and mostly ignoring Hamish unless to give him a strange look and giggle with their hands over their mouths.

This particular evening, however, they had made some effort to speak to him, mostly about school sports day—each time enunciating his name as if there was something peculiarly quaint about it. This was unusual and a little disconcerting.

Eventually, however, Hamish worked out what it was all about. They had discovered that, as a resident, he had a key to the private gardens behind Royal Terrace and they wanted him to let them use the tennis courts there. As soon as Hamish had agreed to this they returned to studiously ignoring him.

Tonight, Hamish intended to conclude the evening with a nightcap—perhaps a twelve-year-old Scapa he had been keeping for a while and retire to bed. But as soon as entering the flat he received a telephone call that changed his plans. Instead, he called a taxi, grabbed the full bottle of Scapa, and locked the door behind him.

Hamish McDavitt arrived at Nigel Stonelaw's house at Little France just before midnight. Little France, on the southern outskirts of Edinburgh, owed its name to its historical connections. It was here that Mary Queen of Scots had maintained her court, of mostly French-speaking nobles, during her years in Edinburgh. Nowadays, however, it was a fairly suburban part of the city, with semis and bungalows, some old farm terraces and, notably, the imposing mass of the new Edinburgh Royal Infirmary, which had decamped here from its original site at Lauriston Place on the edge of the Meadows a couple of years ago.

'It happened this afternoon,' said Nigel. 'I was busy at the office, finishing some paperwork. I'd been camping out at the First and Last pub in Seafield Road for a couple of days hoping to catch some counterfeiters. But nothing came of it. It's been hectic recently, especially with Inspector Rubrik off to his brother's house in Kirkcaldy to attend his mother's funeral.' He paused and took a deep breath. 'Anyway, I had a phone call from a neighbour. Apparently Nora had just

215

collapsed—suddenly, in the street in front of the house. They rushed her to the Infirmary and discovered she had a cyst in the brain. They immediately operated to drain it She's still not conscious. They say the first twelve hours will be critical, I was waiting at the hospital, but they suggested I should come back here as I'm only just across the road.'

'Have you phoned your daughter and her family?' Hamish asked.

'They're on their way, but they were on holiday in West Wales. They're driving up overnight and they should be here early in the morning'. He grimaced and shrugged. 'I just don't know what to do right now.'

Hamish realised that for Nigel, with his fairly brusque and businesslike way of 'getting things done' and a great dislike of hanging about, a situation like this was doubly intolerable.

'Well', he said, 'unfortunately there's not much we can do at the moment. So... ' he placed the bottle he had brought on the table in front of him, 'I think we'll just sit and have a dram until the day dawns.'

Harnish poured a full measure of Scapa into a glass and added an equal measure of water. Nigel's hand was slightly trembling as he handed it to him. He took a large gulp of the whisky which seemed to calm him a little. He looked thoughtful, his eyes a little glazed.

'You lost your wife, didn't you,' Hamish. 'You've never told me about it.'

Hamish wasn't sure that this was an appropriate topic for discussion, but, on the other hand, what else was there? On such an occasion, chatting about work or the weekend's football hardly seemed appropriate

'Yes, well,' Hamish commenced, 'it was some time ago. I

often think about her. Perhaps not every day, but often. And there are dreams. Some happy, some when she seems just to be floating, lost. I think you always will have them, but it is best, I think. Where will the dead reside, if not in the memories of the living? I'm not a religious man, but I suppose I believe that each individual soul remains alive in some way through the effect their life has had on others.'

'Long ago', said Stonelaw, almost dreamily, as he stared into the amber glow of his whisky, 'how long ago was that?'

Hamish drained the last dregs of his glass and refilled them both. He also filled a little milk jug with water from the cold tap and placed it on the table in front of them. He sat back and took a deep breath to compose himself and then he started to tell his story.

'Yes, it was quite some time ago. It was 1959. I had been staying with my aunt and uncle since the death of my mother and father. I attended Anstruther High School and did tolerably well. So I went up to Edinburgh to study English.

'Edinburgh was quite something to me then—a city of opposites: 'the Old Town shuffle and the New Town stride' as it has been called. Auld Reekie, a smoky old city, cold and dark, but full of humanity and life. I shared a flat in Sciennes with two other lads, Bob Sharples and David Lennox. They were studying medicine and chemistry respectively. At first I didn't mell very well with the University crowd. I was just an Ainster Lad, not a city sophisticate, and I didn't play football or rugby or anything like that.

'However, I began to find my way around. I joined the University Hillwalking Club and we went up to the Cairngorms and Glencoe. One year we spent a whole two weeks in Skye and did all of the Cuillin Ridge, bit by bit. I often walked around Edinburgh. I loved to clamber up to the top of Arthur's Seat in the morning and see the whole city laid out before me. I loved Calton Hill too. I'd go up past the Scottish Office and Hill House via the lion steps with the heads of little lions on each boss. Then I'd descend past Royal Terrace, or walk round past Carlton and Regent Terrace, or go down past Croft-an-Righ and back to the Queen's Park.

'Edinburgh was a wonderful place to study literature too. 'Mine ain romantic toun', as Walter Scott called it. You could stroll through the city in the footsteps of Burns or Stevenson. Sometimes we'd go down to Milne's Bar in Rose Street. If you were lucky you would see the poets gather there. Often Norman McCaig or George Mackay Brown and Sydney Goodsir Smith, and occasionally even McDiarmid himself. We never plucked up the courage to speak to them there, but there would be literary events in the Pleasance and around, a lot going on. And, of course, there were the old bookshops: McNaughton's at the top of Leith Walk, and Blackwoods in Dundas Street. I'd spend hours in those browsing, and occasionally there would enough left over from my grant to buy a volume or two

'Then, in my second year, things changed absolutely. That was when I met Liz, Liz Lamont, in the Romantics class with Professor McCorcodale. She was slim with tousled strawberry blond hair and she always seemed to be smiling, We chatted and arranged to have a cup of tea at Teviot Row.

'I can honestly say that the first time I met her I felt as if I had known her all my life. We had so much in common— reading, history, the outdoors. We went on walks together, drank in the Rose Street bars, went to folk sessions and jazz concerts.

'Her family were from Corstorphine, they had a semi at Western Corner. I wouldn't say that they exactly disapproved when we said we wanted to get married. They simply thought that perhaps we should wait until we had finished university, But we were insistent. It was a small ceremony at St Mark's Church, with a reception afterwards at the Dowager House. Neither of us had extended families and we only invited a few close friends from University

'We rented a small flat in Polwarth and studied for our finals. Shortly afterwards, however, only eleven months after we were married, Liz was killed in a road accident.'

Nigel was still staring into his whisky, which Hamish looked up. 'Is that the end, then. Another tragic accident and nothing to be done about it.' He looked forlorn, and then realised that his blunt statement may have seemed insensitive.

'Oh, I'm sorry, Hamish, I mean… '

'No, not quite', said Hamish, 'Of course it *was* the end. There was nothing I could do to recover her. If only I was Orpheus and could venture into the Underworld and win her back. No, the pain lasted for a very long time. But I had to get on. I left the University. A new life was beginning, but the old one had gone, Far too soon. I was still barely a man.

'But, after the accident, I thought… Well, I didn't know what to think, whether to try to forget everything or move somewhere else. But something inside me forced me on. I had to know what happened that night. I had—have always believed that the truth must be faced, however difficult it may be to do so.

'You see, what happened was that on the night that Liz died, she had arranged to go out with some of her old school friends. We had just finished our exams. We were exhausted with all the studying, I was going on the same night to the Students' Union with my flatmates from my first year and some other friends I had made in Edinburgh, but Liz had arranged a girls' night out. They were going to have a drink in the Forresthill Bar then go down to the West End Café, next to the milk bar at the West End, to hear some jazz. There was Liz and three of her chums from school—there was Cilla Peatsfield, her parents had a farm out at Haddington, She was studying history. Then there was Daisy Livingstone, whose parents were quite well off and had a townhouse in Cumberland Street. She was studying English and drama. And there was Penelope Pound who used to claim that she was related to the poet Ezra Pound. Her father, who was divorced, was a businessman and very nouveau riche, She lived with him in a detached house in Colinton. She was studying law, although we all felt that she was struggling with it. They had all gone to James Gillespie's School for Girls. You may have heard of it. It was the school immortalised by Muriel Spark's novel, *The Prime of Miss Jean Brodie*.

'They had been as tight as tuppence, studying, playing hockey, passing notes and little drawings to each other in class, smoking Lucky Strikes behind the lavatories. All the things that girls get up to. They had always kept in touch, seeing each other at least once a week since they left school. What exactly happened that night is not quite clear. All we know is that they were all quite tipsy by the time they got to the West End. Apparently, when they were coming out of the West End Café, Liz apparently went over on a heel and lurched on the pavement in front of a bus. She was rushed to hospital, but she had suffered a severe injury to the head and died that night, before her parents, who were at a concert that night, or I could be contacted.

'That was it. The funeral was five days later. Strangely, I remember it vividly, but only in parts. I was so numb that other parts have been quite forgotten. My memories now are almost as if watching an edited videotape, at a distance. Then afterwards… well, it was over. And yet, I wasn't satisfied. Liz was always very level-headed. More so than me. Even if she had had a few drinks, I couldn't believe that she would let herself get so much out of control as to stagger in front of a bus. I spoke to her friends, but the details they remembered were elusive and unhelpful.

'Eventually, I went back to our flat and looked through her personal things. I didn't really know what I was looking for or why I was doing it, but maybe I thought there must be a clue of some sort. Something which would explain what had happened. It was maybe a stupid thing to do, but it was all I could do. What else did I have?

'I was there for one, two, three days. I can't honestly remember. I didn't eat, and if I slept, it was only intermittently, Eventually, I found letters she had kept—from her school friends. People wrote a lot more those days. They exchanged letters during school holidays, when they were at their parents for weekends, even notes when they were at school together. The letters were often cryptic, as young girls will write letters, referring to gossip or little incidents that they thought important. Sometimes, they indicated friends by nicknames or personal epithets. They often included little drawings or symbols in the margins or at the end.

'I read them time and time again. Sometimes I felt I was intruding into private lives, but also I felt that it brought me closer to Liz, to her life before she met me. You may think it was a morbid task, but I only found life in it.'

Hamish had become quite animated trying to explain this, but now he sat back in his chair, quite composed and spoke slowly and carefully.

'It was the first mystery that I ever solved and, in a way, the last. The last because everything would now change. Something that was part of me had to die too. What happened was that, eventually, after I had read the letters over many times, the characters—people—in them became real to me in a way that perhaps no one else would understand. And I was sure that I had identified a pattern. In the letters from the person who signed herself 'DL', there seemed to me an undercurrent of jealousy and spitefulness that would not necessarily be detected by the reader initially. To heighten my suspicions, there was a reference in a letter signed 'PP' to an anonymous figure who, as the sender of the letter wrote to Liz, is 'having a little fury against you'.

'I had no doubt, 'DL' had a grudge against Liz. Why, I don't know. Perhaps she was prettier, more successful, more at ease in company. Even perhaps, and I hesitated to think about it, because she had married me or... '

Stonelaw, who had been listening intently, suddenly sat forward in his chair. 'So... it must have been Daisy. Daisy Livingstone. The letter signed 'PP'—from Penelope Pound—gives it away! Did you ask Penelope, She could have confirmed it!'

Hamish shook his head. 'No, in fact that would have been a bad mistake.'

He continued. "PP" was, of course, Cilla... Priscilla Peatsfield. Daisy never signed herself 'DL'. She always finished her letters with a little flower—a daisy. I mentioned the drawings and symbols they used to use.'

Stonelaw seemed perplexed. 'So, who was 'DL' then?'

'That was what puzzled me, but then I worked it out. You're old enough, Nigel. You must remember when you were at school. Arithmetic wasn't quite so easy then as it is now! There were twelve pennies to a shilling, twenty shillings to a pound. Twenty-one shillings to a guinea. I used to love the old coins, tanners, florins, threepenny bits with twelve sides, halfpennies with an old sailing ship on the back. I collected bun pennies, from the early years of Queen Victoria's reign, so-called because of the bun style of her hair. It was wonderful—all that history to be found in a pocketful of change.'

Stonelaw still looked puzzled and Hamish decided to get to the point

'L. S. D. Librae… solidi… denarii. Pounds, shillings, pence. Penny Pound, 'DL', pennies, pounds. That was her pet way of signing herself.'

'Ah… ' Nigel suddenly understood. 'I see!' He took a gulp of his whisky and seemed about to say something else. But he stopped, glanced towards the window and then back at Hamish, and then we took some more whisky, but just a sip, flexing as if it was bitter to his tongue. 'So what did you do?'

'Well, I confronted her. It seemed all I could do. She admitted it right away. Guilt had been preying on her mind. She had started taking the drugs herself in small doses. It helped her get through her classes with which she was struggling. She was always jealous of Liz and she was particularly stressed that night because she expected she had flunked her exams. She had spiked Liz's drink out of spite. She thought she might make a fool of herself in front of the others. She regretted it now. And that was it.'

'And what did you do then? Did you report the matter to the police. They could have done something.'

'No, that wouldn't have helped. There was nothing to do. Penny Pound didn't intend to kill Liz. There are a few people who are irredeemably evil—you and I have perhaps come across some of those—but most people are a mixture of good and bad. However, more importantly, their actions can have consequences that can be both good and bad, sometimes far beyond their intentions. Penelope Pound was not necessarily a bad person—just insecure and jealous and foolish. She had to live with the consequences of her actions as well as I.'

'Were you not angry? Did you not want revenge?'

'Oh yes, I was very angry for a long time, but not angry enough to do anything silly. As we get older, death becomes more acceptable. We have seen more of it. Hopefully, as we get older we are more forgiving, we see that anger and jealousy and the lust for revenge are part of the source of evil itself. They destroy everything they come in contact with. I hope that Penelope Pound learned that in time herself?'

'And that was the end of it?'

'Yes, we all moved on somehow. After I graduated I got a job at the Edinburgh Central Library, in the Edinburgh Room. I moved out of the flat in Polwarth and stayed in Forrest Road for a while. Cilla became a schoolmistress and was quite successful, ending up as an assistant head teacher back at James Gillespie's. She married later in life and had twin girls. Daisy... well Daisy, as Muriel Spark herself might have said, became famous for sex! She moved into the theatre, then television presenting, had three husbands and was always in the glamour pages of the popular press.'

'I suppose that you never saw Penny Pound again,' said Stonelaw, 'I wonder whatever happened to her?'

'I never saw her, but I know what happened to her. Edinburgh is such a small place! She failed her finals and didn't go back to university, and then, quite suddenly, a few months later, she married a Polish immigrant, who had a business selling shoes. Eventually, she became a midwife and he opened his own shoe store in Leith Walk. They had two sons, I believe, before the husband died of heart failure. And Penny was to follow him.'

'She died then?'

'Yes, very recently—of cancer. I saw the intimation in the *Daily Scot* just the other day: 'Penelope Rubrik, née Pound.'

Stonelaw started in astonishment. 'Rubrik!'

'Yes, I believe that you know her younger son.'

'Inspector Rubrik!' Stonelaw had always underestimated Hamish's ability to surprise him. 'Does he know about this?'

'I don't know. I hope not. As far as I can tell only you and I know this little story. It is in the past and perhaps it should be forgotten. Unfortunately, however, not all of us are always as good as we would wish at the art of forgetting.'

Hamish arose from the sofa, realising that his legs were stiff and sleepy from sitting so long. He went over to the window and opened the curtain, letting in a surprising beam of sunshine. At the same time, they both heard a crunch of gravel as a car pulled into the drive.

'We've been chatting so long over our whiskies that it's dawn,' he said. 'Our vigil is nearly over. It looks like a fine day and, now that twelve hours have passed and gone, I hope that soon there may be some very good news!'

And once again, Hamish McDavitt was right!

forthcoming

The Munro Murders

'Hold on, what exactly are Munros?' asked Detective Inspector Nigel Stonelaw.

'Oh, that's obvious. They're Scottish mountains over 3000 feet high,' replied Hamish McDavitt.

'And you say that three murders have been committed on the three biggest, and that someone might be responsible for them all?' 'Yes.' Stonelaw's brow was creased.

'And how many of these Munros are there altogether?'

'Two hundred and eighty two.'

'Good God,' said Stonelaw, that would be the most serial killings since... since... ' And further words completely failed him.